The Whale's Way

Heather Kellerhals-Stewart

Illustrations by John Hodges

POLESTAR
BOOK PUBLISHERS

Published by
Polestar Press Ltd., R.R. 1, Winlaw, B.C., V0G 2J0, 604 226-7670

Distributed in the United States by
Slawson Communications Inc., 165 Vallecitos De Oro,
San Marcos, CA 92069 619 744-2299

Published with the assistance of the Canada Council and the
B.C. Cultural Services Branch

Canadian Cataloguing in Publication Data
Kellerhals-Stewart, Heather, 1937-
The whale's way
ISBN 0-919591-30-2

I. Hodges, John, 1941-   II. Title.
PS8571.E45W4 1988   jC813'.54   C88-091499-8
PZ7.K445Wh 1988

Cover and interior illustrations by John Hodges

The Whale's Way was edited by Stephanie Judy, typeset by Julian Ross,
and designed by Jim Brennan.

Printed in Canada

Acknowledgements

Thanks to

Stephanie Judy for patient help with the manuscript, Julian Ross
for his wonderful encouragement, Dr. Paul Rosseau of Quadra
Island for advice and suggested reading on autistic children,
Rolf Kellerhals for scouring the manuscript and helping with the
map, the Society of Authors as the literary representative of the
Estate of John Masefield, and the staff of the Vancouver Public
Aquarium for answering my many, many questions.

*To Rolf, Erika, Markus, Angy, Flora and Solo
and the many good times together on Quadra*

Sea Fever

I must down to the seas again, to the lonely seas and the sky,
And all I ask is a tall ship and a star to steer her by,
And the wheel's kick and the wind's song and the white
    sail's shaking,
And a grey mist on the sea's face and a grey dawn breaking.

I must down to the seas again, for the call of the running tide
Is a wild call and a clear call that may not be denied;
And all I ask is a windy day with the white clouds flying,
And the flung spray and the blown spume, and the
    sea-gulls crying.

I must down to the seas again to the vagrant gypsy life,
To the gull's way and the whale's way where the wind's
    like a whetted knife;
And all I ask is a merry yarn from a laughing fellow rover,
And quiet sleep and a sweet dream when the long trick's over.

John Masefield

BRITISH
COLUMBIA

Coast Mountains

Johnstone Strait

Robson
Bight

Vancouver Island

~ Pacific Ocean ~

N

0   50   100
        km

~ Strait of Georgia ~

Vancouver

U.S.A.

~ Juan de Fuca Strait ~

Victoria

Seattle

Vancouver Island

Discovery Passage

Quadra Island

Jesse's home

School

Read Island

Woody and Sal

Cortes Island

Cape Mudge Lighthouse

0   5   10
km

Raza's Story

Far up in Johnstone Strait, between Vancouver Island and the British Columbia mainland, a killer whale pod was swimming south. There were two males, a female about to give birth to a calf and one youngster. Other killer whale groups remained in the Strait most of the year, but this was a transient pod in strange waters and they seemed hurried.

They pressed past the fish boats that were setting out nets for salmon. They ignored the cries of other whales and the screeching of sea gulls overhead. The noise and confusion of boats made the old ones jumpy. These waters were dangerous. Before the birth of the calf they must find a more sheltered place.

11

But the youngster, Raza, had a mind of his own. The throb of boat engines, the excited clicks and cries of the strange whales, the swish of fish nets, were all sounds to investigate. Certainly not to rush past!

"Wheee," he whistled. His cry bounced off the hull of a trawler that was pulling in its nets.

"Something interesting here — lots of salmon," the echo back told him. Raza shot past the old ones, almost landing in the middle of the nets.

"Something dangerous here, trawler, humans." Back came the oldest bull's information. With a sudden burst of speed that propelled him through the air, he knocked Raza off course and for good measure slapped the youngster with his flipper.

"Old-stick-in-the-sand," Raza grumbled. "No fun, no nothing!"

For a while he lingered behind the others, letting the current do most of the work. Sometimes it felt like a smooth stream sliding over his skin. Let the others rush on. He preferred to take his time and enjoy the scene. Every so often he blurted out a few angry clicks to echo-locate himself. Not that he really cared where the others were or what they were doing. Someday he would be a powerful orca, ranging far and wide over the whole ocean. Free!

"Raza," came the sudden roar, "you're falling too far behind. You will soon be out of sound range. Hurry up. We're waiting at dot, dot, dash, click..." and the bull gave him the exact location.

Raza swept his powerful tail flukes through the water. He'd show those old ones a trick or two. With a tremendous burst of speed he shot above the water — all four meters of his gleaming black and white body. Can't fool around with this orca! Someday he would outleap them all. And as for lobtailing, why he was an expert already. Raza rolled onto his back and by smacking his tail flukes on the surface, propelled himself forward.

Suddenly he stopped and swerved to the right. After many kilometers of straight shoreline, here at last was a dent in the coast. Sounds were coming from the bight — sounds of whales rolling, splashing and rubbing their backs on the rocks near the shore. Were they playing or what? Raza couldn't understand a squeak of what the stranger whales were saying. Trust the old ones to have swum right past. Any time things began to look the least bit interesting...

Raza spyhopped, popping his head clear of the water to orient himself. Sometimes it was good to know how things looked as well as how they sounded. And what Raza saw was very, very interesting. There were many small boats in the bight, some of them looking more like slivers of logs floating on the surface. Raza swam closer to investigate.

"Click...click." A sudden burst of sound came from the old bull. "I want your exact location, Raza. Now."

"Squee!" In spite of being inside the bight he wasn't out of sound range. Old stick-in-the-sand was like an octopus with tentacles that wouldn't mind their own business. At that very moment he was probably reversing course and swimming back to find him, which meant no more fun exploring.

"Whoosh." Raza surfaced near one of the boats to take a quick breath. You could never be sure of boats or humans. With seals and sea lions and salmon and sea gulls you got to know their every move off by heart. The old ones always made a wide detour around boats.

"Wouldn't they be furious to see me this close to one," Raza thought. It looked harmless enough. But just in case,

13

he sent a location message to old bull. "Find me in bay, past rocky point. Coming soon."

Then Raza dove underneath the boat. Strange! The very message that he had sent to old bull was coming back to him from the boat. What was going on here? It sounded like his own voice, yet somehow different. He repeated the squeals and whistles and for good measure added a trill at the end. Back came the message with the extra trill. Although it made no sense, something exciting, something stupendous was happening here. Shivers wriggled over Raza's skin. It was the same feeling he got when swimming below a storm, or floating with the full moon overhead.

Blam! The old whale rammed Raza in the side, knocking the breath out of him and rolling him away from the boat.

"What have I told you, time and time again, about approaching humans?" the old bull roared.

"But the sounds," Raza squeaked, "the sounds are too interesting. We can't leave now."

"Come, before it's too late," the old one said more softly. "We shall never understand humans."

"But...something was about to happen. There are other whales here. It isn't that dangerous. Can't we stay?"

"No! These are stranger whales in a strange place. Here nothing happens in the old, familiar way. I've heard rumours sifting through the sea of humans sending messages and imitating our voices... wishful, dangerous thinking! Come Raza, before it is too late."

For an instant the old one lingered, listening to the stranger whales, rolling and splashing near the beach. Their sounds filled the ocean and overflowed into the sky. Raza shivered again. Although it frightened him, he didn't want to leave.

"Now go," the old whale whistled. "We are only passers-by here. We don't belong in this place and never will."

Raza fell in line with the rest of his pod who were hovering outside the bight. His side still ached where the old bull had rammed him. Except to chase after a dog fish, he never swerved off course once.

The sun fell behind the mountains of Vancouver Island, but still the female had not found a resting place to her liking. Raza noticed she was swimming slower, sticking her head into every crack and corner of the coastline. Why couldn't she make up her mind? All he needed was a place — any place — where he could stop to rest his aching side.

Shortly before nightfall the pod swerved towards an inlet. Raza listened as the others paused at the entrance to gain their bearings. "Click, click, click..." Back came the sonar picture — long, narrow inlet, lagoon at end, reef ahead, but depth adequate.

Still the old ones hesitated, listening to the tide roar into the lagoon. Tides pour out as well as in, and water levels could drop sharply. But the female groaned again. Seeing there was no time to lose, the pod nosed cautiously forward, letting the tide push and finally spill them into the lagoon.

Sometime early in the morning the calf was born. Raza heard the squeaks and whistles and saw the baby's tail flapping from the female's underside while its head was still inside.

"Wheee!" Raza whistled and skimmed around the surface of the lagoon. After he calmed down, he joined the others who were pushing the baby to the surface, helping it to breathe.

"Barely half the size of me," Raza gloated.

Already the old bull was fussing about the tide-fall. "Go, Raza, and sound the inlet. Swim dead centre where the water is deepest and check the depth as you proceed, taking care to steer clear of the reef. Listen to the tide-fall from a distance, then return and report."

Sent on an errand by you-know-who and about time! He was beginning to wonder how old he'd have to be before being trusted with an important job. "Wheee... this is more like it."

Raza smacked his tail flukes on the tide riffles as he swam down the inlet. Every moment or so he slowed to test the depth. "Click, click...clearance at least two meters. Full speed ahead."

Although the boulders lining the edge of the inlet loomed closer in the falling tide, there was still room to slip through or even turn around with care. But listen, up ahead! The tide was pouring over the reef like a wild river, swirling the water into whirlpools. One last forward sweep, no further. The roar filled his head, the current caught him unawares. Too late, too late to turn...Raza tried, but each time lost more ground. The rapids sucked him down, then threw him clear, with only a scratch on the belly to show.

Raza sucked air into his bursting lungs. One thing he knew now — the others were too big to pass over the reef. They must wait for the turn of the tide. And meanwhile he was trapped outside, alone...

Raza imagined the old bull's nagging. "What keeps that youngster, Raza? Too young and careless for such a task. I should have gone myself."

Raza squirmed. "I'm not too young or careless." It was plain, bad luck. It could have happened to anyone, even old bull himself. If only he could get a message back to the others!

Raza spyhopped to gain his bearings. Through the grey-ness of the morning he spied a light, a human fire near the entrance to the inlet. There was danger lurking there perhaps, but company also in the early morning, lonely time.

He swam closer to investigate. "Click, click...large boat moored near shore, smaller one dragged onto beach. Watch it — shallow water ahead." Raza surfaced to breathe. "Whoosh!"

The three men sitting around the fire jumped to their feet. Raza could hear the shouts. Forgetting the old bull's warnings, he went closer still and smacked his tail flukes on the water. "My whoosh surprised them, that's what!"

"Hey Vic," came one of the voices. "Take a look at that little killer. Where do you think he came from?"

"Down the inlet," Vic replied, "or we'd have noticed his blowing earlier. I've seen whales in the lagoon before. Probably a pod there now."

"Yeah? The inlet seems like a funny place for whales to go, being so narrow. I bet the little guy is a stray."

"While you two argue it out, I'm going to see for myself," the third man said. "And maybe catch a killer whale or two."

"Relax, Fred, unless you're looking for trouble. You need a permit nowadays to capture a killer whale. Times have changed since you took that whale a while back."

"Look, Vic, don't tell me what to do. I plan to run the skiff up the inlet, stretch our old fish net across the lagoon entrance and with luck I'll hold those whales. There's still money in killers — plenty, if you know the right people and keep your mouth shut."

"Sure, Fred, and a heap of trouble too. Ever seen a pod react when it's separated? Pure dynamite. You may hold them for a while, but the big ones will loosen things up for you, especially when they hear the little fellow out here squealing his head off."

"Maybe this will scare the little beggar away." Fred grabbed his .22 rifle from the skiff and started firing.

Raza dove, but not fast enough to avoid the wildly flying bullets. The first one grazed his back, the second lodged in his tail flukes. Was he even safe below? He could hear the explosions shattering the surface above him. So this was what the old ones feared! His back stung from the bullet's course, but worse by far than the hurt was the deadly fear. No matter which way he zigzagged or circled, the red streamer flowing from his back followed him like some ghostly tracker. Raza panicked...the others from his pod, old bull, he must get back to them.

Raza charged up the inlet, almost smashing into the reef. The water barely covered the rocks. Before high tide surged across that reef again, the sun must sink in the western sky. But what if the terrible explosions followed him up the inlet, trapping him against the rocks? What if they were coming now? I'll leap across the reef. They will never catch me alive. "I'm coming," Raza squealed, "I'm coming."

"Don't jump, Raza." The old bull's voice touched him as though they were lying side by side under the peaceful moon. "Let go of your fear, Raza. There are worse things than being alone for a time. Swim over the ocean and far away and don't return to look for us here. Listen...I hear a boat moving up the inlet. Swim for your life, Raza...swim."

The old bull was so close Raza could hear the water lapping against his dorsal fin. A mere spitful of water away on the other side of the reef!

"No, don't," the powerful voice warned again. "Even I

could not leap across this reef."

"Same old stick-in-the-sand, always boasting, always nosing his way into somebody else's thoughts." Raza shot a mouthful of water across the reef. Splat! It hit the old bull in the eye.

"That's the spirit, Raza. Think like an orca, act like an orca. Now go and till we meet again, farewell."

Raza sucked air through his blowhole till he thought his head would split. It had to last him all the way down the inlet. Then silently he submerged himself and like a shadow stole beneath the rocks rising from the water.

The skiff was directly above him now. Raza could see the shape and hear the oars biting into the water. So easy to toss that shape, smash it and grind it into a million grains of sand. A quiver ran down Raza's back. Who was the hunter now? But Raza swam on and the oars rose and fell until the skiff was out of hearing.

The entrance to the inlet was still a long way off. Raza's lungs were bursting, his head was splitting — he must surface soon for air. Old bull would never be gasping for air like this. Stay down, stay down.... Look, the channel widens, deepens, the giant kelp fronds lose their grip ahead.... And Raza smashed to the surface, blowing.

More than a kilometer away, the old bull, standing guard by the reef, heard the sound. The hunter heard it too and swore. But Raza was gone, heading southeast with the old one's call echoing around him. "Swim over the ocean and far away. Swim for your life, Raza. And don't return to look for us here."

Flora's Story

Outside the potato sack which had brought her to the island, the grey goose could hear the chatter of other geese.

"Is it one of us, is it?"

"Probably, probably."

"Whatever it is I'm terribly, terribly curious."

"Me too, me too."

"Look out, look out! It's coming down."

Someone lifted the sack from the back of the pickup truck, jerked the rope loose and shook the grey goose into a bright, spring afternoon. She blinked. Standing around the truck in a semicircle were the other geese — all white. Theirs was the whiteness of daisy petals at dawn, of sun-washed waves, of moth wings in the moonlight. The grey goose's greyness clung to her like a wet blanket. She shook the dust and potato roots from her feathers. This was worse than emerging from the egg.

"Gr...greetings," she stammered.

"Howdy-do, howdy-do. She must mean howdy-do."

"On closer inspection her complexion is terrible."

"Terribly, terribly plain."

"Just look at her brown eyes," one of the blue-eyed geese hissed. "Do you think she can see anything?"

"We dubiously, dubiously doubt it."

"Of course I can see," the grey goose protested. "Blue eyes, brown eyes, grey eyes, mauve eyes, fluorescent eyes...it's simply a colour matter.

"She talks funny, frabulously funny."

From underneath the truck came a whimper. "Are you by any chance, if you don't mind my asking, a dog-loving goose?"

"I beg your pardon. A what?" the grey goose asked.

"Not so loud or the other geese will hear us talking. I said a dog-loving goose."

"I'd say dog-loving is a bit far fetched. How about dog-tolerating or dog-liking, for starters?"

"You don't nip dog's ears or latch onto their tails?"

"Almost never, unless provoked into direct and sudden action."

The white geese spotted the dog. "Grab her, nab her, bite him. Make him smart and throb."

"You know what, know what?" they jabbered.

"She talks to dogs. DOGS."

"Utterly, utterly common."

Two kids came running up to the truck.

"So how do you like the new goose?" Mr. Fredricksen asked his twins.

"Kind of low-slung," Woody replied. "Is she loaded with eggs or something?"

"I certainly hope so. That's why I bought her."

Woody wrinkled his nose. "I'm not eating any. They're too huge and sticky."

"Don't worry, Woody. Any spare eggs are going straight into the incubator. I want goslings this summer, hundreds of goslings."

"Flora," Sal said dreamily. "I think I'll call her Flora."

Woody groaned. "Do you have to give ridiculous names to every little bird and beetle around the farm?"

"I look after the geese. I can do what I like."

"Who cares! They'll have their heads chopped off in the fall. Ask Dad."

"That's enough you two."

"Dad, you couldn't..."

"Sal, they are a year old, prime time for a goose. The ones that don't lay eggs and raise goslings this summer will have to go."

"I told you so..."

"What did I say, Woody? And my advice for you, Sal, is to stop crossing all your bridges before you get to them. Who knows what fall will bring?"

"Lots of bust bridges," Sal grumbled under her breath.

"What an introduction!" Flora murmured, as she nestled down in the warm sand to preen and peck her feathers into place.

The other geese watched from a safe distance.

"Will she stay?"

"Probably, probably."

"Better believe it."

Flora curled her head under one wing, pretending to be asleep, until the other geese grew bored and waddled off.

The longest day of the year burst into summer and still there were no goslings. Already the crickets were warning

23

everybody of time passing — one singer by the barn door, a second in the woodshed, a third under the kitchen mop.... Soon it would be a chorus.

> *Swing low*
> *Sunglow.*
> *Swing slow*
> *Summer goes.*
> *Swing, sing,*
> *Sing, swing.*
> *Long ago —*
> *To and fro,*
> *To and fro —*
> *Time to go...*

But the eggs kept disappearing as soon as they were laid.

"Lay 'em bigger, better," the white geese honked.

"After extensive investigation I have discovered that your problem lies with the ravens," Flora tried to explain. "Everytime you leave your nests for a bite of grass, a raven swoops down and snatches an egg. Try camouflaging your nests with twigs or grass."

The white geese turned their heads sideways and stared at the ravens riding the warm updraft along the cliff.

"Who knows? Who knows?"

"Certainly not her, certainly not."

"Back to work — bigger, better."

Naturally Mr. Fredricksen blamed the dog. "Developed a taste for goose yolk, have you? We'll fix that." He rubbed his nose in the shattered remains of an egg and locked him in the tool shed. "Bad, bad, dog!"

"You shouldn't accuse her without a scrap of evidence," the twins protested, agreeing for once.

Flora sat herself down in front of the shed and hissed

whenever Mr. Fredricksen walked past. Every few moments she proclaimed her friend's innocence to the world. "You see here one innocent dog, unjustly accused. You have here one innocent dog..."

"Breakdown, breakin, breakage," the white geese honked.

Nobody was sure who or what they meant, but the uproar worked. Mr. Fredricksen let the dog go free.

"Darn kids and animals," he grumbled, "I'd like to get rid of them all."

The twins helped him hang some fish netting around the nests to keep out prowlers, but it was too late. The geese had started quarreling. They quarreled about nests, they quarreled about eggs, they laid eggs in the wrong place, they rolled eggs from one nest to another and they even managed to break their own eggs.

"I smell trouble," Flora said to her friend one morning.

"Actually I'm sniffing rotten eggs," the dog replied. And he was right. The eggs were putrefying. Mr. Fredricksen stepped on one and it exploded like a balloon. The stink almost overpowered him.

"Wow, some eggs-plosion!" Woody sniggered.

"Very funny, Woody!"

By the end of summer there were bits and pieces of egg shell scattered all over the farm.

There was a change coming on. Flora felt it and so did everyone else, with the exception of Woody who was too busy building the last of his summer rafts to notice anything.

Flora watched the white geese flapping overhead. If only it was the real thing — a genuine migration. But they were doing this four, maybe five times a day now. Waddle, shuffle, scuttle. Clear the runway. Look out! Runaway, runaway. Take off, take off. Veering left — the tree, the tree — watch that tree! On course again, on course.

Belly-flop in the bay and waddle back up hill to begin all over again.

"What a bore!" Flora sighed. She waddled over to inspect Mr. Fredricksen's latest project.

Sal was there arguing with him. "Dad, it's too early to be cleaning the butchering barrel."

"Barrels get rusty and spring leaks over winter you know, Sal."

"It's too early to kill the geese."

"To everything there is a season..." Mr. Fredricksen muttered, "a time to plant and a time to pick..."

"Dad, you're not paying attention."

"How can I concentrate when you're dancing around me like a mosquito? The fact is there's hardly any green grass left for the geese to eat and the first cool day that comes along we ought to butcher them."

Flora plumped herself down on Sal's bare feet. Had she felt a cold wind stirring in the northwest?

"But it's not fair, just because a bit of weather comes along..."

"Nothing is completely fair, Sal, least of all our weather."

Seconds later the bare feet ran away and Flora felt a cold nose nudging her feathers.

"I heard everything," the dog whimpered. "I'm trying to think up a getaway plan, but my brain keeps shivering. If only my brain was as smart as my nose. Achoo! It's growing colder — I can feel it."

"Pull yourself together, please. Nobody is planning to chop off your head."

"But they might kill you if we don't find a plan and you're my one and only friend. Achoo!"

"Do stop this snivelling and sneezing or my brain will atrophy."

"What's a - trophy?"

"My brain will shrivel up and die."

The dog stopped sneezing. "I wouldn't want that to happen."

"Good. Now if you'll be kind enough to leave me alone so I can contemplate this urgent problem..."

Flora waddled over to the goose run and pecked half heartedly at a few leftover grains of barley. What was the point of eating? She'd only grow plumper and more attractive for the slaughter. Thank goodness the other geese weren't around. They were still busy trying to migrate.

Evening came early and with it a cold wind from the northwest. As the lights in the house went off one by one, the night creatures began to stir. A bat rustled over the goose run, a tree frog sang its cautious chorus, a wolf howled from the far hills.... The white geese murmured sleepily and pressed closer together. Only Flora stood alone.

It struck without warning, without a sound, without a moon to light the way. The blow knocked Flora off her feet and rolled her down the slope. A knife-like thing raked across her chest. She felt the blood oozing through her feathers. Too stunned to shriek, she beat her wings against the thing — again and again and again. The strokes could break a hand or arm, but still the knife-like, sharpened hooks held on. Flora gasped for breath against the weight that pressed her down.

"It's trouble," the other geese jabbered, gathering in a circle around Flora. "Terrible, terrible trouble."

Between the beating of her wings, Flora saw a light snap on in the house. Or was the flash in her own head, the final flash of light before she died?

"Trouble, we have trouble here. Oh yes, trouble."

A flashlight bobbed through the darkness. Sal...she was coming to pull the terrible, tearing thing away.

"Flora, stop whacking yourself with your own wings. Have you gone crazy? Shove off you other geese and let me by."

"We told you so, truthfully, truthfully so. There's trouble here, trouble."

"Shut up you silly geese. And if you aren't careful with that flapping wing, Flora, you'll break my arm."

Sal grabbed a wing or something and shone her flashlight at the catch. "You won't believe it. I've got someone else's feathers here."

In the flashlight's beam Flora saw two yellow eyes glaring up at her.

"An owl," Sal whispered, "a great horned owl. He can't carry you off and he can't tear his talons loose, so you're both trapped."

"Trapped spells trouble. Double, double, trouble," the other geese chorused.

"Oh go way," Sal scolded. "If I don't pry them loose they'll kill each other for sure. Hold on, Flora. I'll fetch a broom."

Flora watched the flashlight bob over to the shed. Hurry... those fierce, yellow eyes were everywhere. What if they were draining the last drops of blood from her body? Hurry, hurry, no time to waste. And now Sal was back, pushing and prying with the broom, trying to loosen the owl's fierce grip. Push harder, harder...

"Oof!" As the talons came loose Sal and Flora tumbled into the muck of the goose run.

Slowly, very slowly, the great horned owl limped away. The yellow eyes turned and glared back at them, before vanishing into the fir trees.

"She's dangerous, probably contagious," the white geese hissed.

"She's not one of us. Certainly, certainly not."

28

"Broom her out. Broom her out."

Flora felt Sal lifting her, then tucking her into the musty hay of the old dog house. "Better stay here for the rest of the night. I don't trust those other geese."

Gradually everyone settled back to sleep, except the grey goose, who waited until it was time to leave. There was no choice. It if wasn't an owl or an axe, something else would surely fall upon her head. And it would always be so, for she stood alone, apart from the flock.

Yes, it's time to go. Flora uncurled her feet from the warm hole in the hay and flapped her wings. Stiff and aching all over, but still workable. Now if she could slip past the dog without raising a ruckus.

"Who goes there?" the small voice snuffled.

"A friend. But don't disturb the other geese or they will honk everybody awake."

"You're leaving, aren't you?" the dog whimpered. "All night long my nose and ears have been telling me the bad news."

"Yes, I'm setting sail with the northwest wind at my back and by morning I should be far out to sea."

"Remember to keep one eye open for seals and sea lions and other things from below. And don't waggle your flippers for all the world to see."

"I'll keep a sharp lookout," Flora promised. "Au revoir, my friend, till we meet again."

All she heard was a snuffle in the darkness.

Flora tested the water with one webbed foot. Cold, even for a goose's leg, and dark and dreary as the insides of a potato sack. With the water lapping against her feathers, she shoved off and let the wind do the rest. The grey goose was afloat, with the northwest wind taking her past the first point, past Seal Island, past the navigation buoy...

Setting sail into the dark without a friend is hard, she

thought. Was that a howl coming from the far off land?

"Keep an eye open for seals and sea lions and don't waggle your flippers for all the world to see," came the warning.

Flora tried not to think about the things lurking below. There was enough to worry about on the surface, thank you very much. Already her legs were turning a brighter shade of orange from the cold. She tucked them inside her feathers. "There, you're warmer and nicely camouflaged too."

To keep herself awake she recited rhymes,

> *One, two, tickle my toes,*
> *Three, four, frazzle my feet...*

But very softly, so nobody would hear and call her silly.

Let the wind do what it will and carry the grey goose over the waves and far away...the poor, grey goose...

Raza & Flora

"Swim over the ocean and far away. Swim for your life, Raza. And don't return to look for us here."

And Raza swam east and southeast along Johnstone Strait, with the old bull's echo following him like a dolphin after a ship at sea. By evening he was...

Raza stopped in the middle of a forward stroke to listen. It felt too quiet. Where was the echo from his pod? "Squee, whee, where am I?"

No reply. Was he off course? Had anything terrible happened to his pod or was he forgetting how they sounded? Although the current still swirled past Raza it carried nothing except his own excited squeals.

"Think like an orca, act like an orca."

There, the echo came again. So he could bring it back

when he wanted. But how does an orca act? I can't think properly all alone. I can't remember. Even the water flowing over my skin feels different. "Where am I?"

I'll echo-locate myself, that's what. "Click, click?" Big boulder to my right. Back eddy. Quiet place to rest.

First sensible answer all evening! Raza patted himself on the side with one flipper. Hungry though and very, very tired. Stiff and hurting all over.

Splash! Two shapes slithered off the boulder.

"Wait, don't go. I'd like company."

"Sure, you'd like company," the harbour seals replied, "some company in your great, cavernous stomach. We know your kind."

"No, wait. I'm all alone. I don't want to eat you. I'm too tired to chase anything."

"Yeah? Tell that to our sister who got swallowed by a pack of killers."

Too late. They'd gone. And who cared? Rotten company by their sound. Now he had the back eddy all to himself. A chinook salmon blundered in and Raza swallowed it whole. "Hmm...good, more like an orca now."

The wash from the back eddy soothed his aching back. All he had to do was lie still and let it swirl him slowly, round and round. Better than fighting the tidal current out there. Raza stared gloomily at the strait. The coast was squeezing it from both sides. More boats and less room to steer. Dangerous. Look at the scars on my back. That's what humans do.

A deep throbbing filled the back eddy, vibrating through Raza's jaw, where he collected sounds, and down his backbone. Humans and their boats again! And by the noise, a tugboat pulling trees. How many times had the old ones warned him to steer clear of logbooms?

A flock of herring gulls were hitching a ride on the boom.

"Killer, baby killer in that back eddy," they squawked, "but he doesn't amount to a hill of seaweed."

"Squee...garbage breath," Raza whistled. "If you didn't taste so bad I'd swallow you one by one."

"Little, baby killer whale — can't catch us."

Gulls, he hated them. Noisy, big-mouthed, stealers of food. Raza smacked his tail flukes on the water. Why was that boom taking so long to pass?

Sometime during the night the steady thump, thump, thump of a diesel engine moved down the strait. So familiar was the noise it scarcely entered Raza's dream of leaping, lobtailing, speed swimming, but another sound shook him wide awake. What was it? Wilder than the cry of the winter loon, sweeter and more mysterious than the cry of the stranger whales it came.

"Click, click?"

Large ship travelling down strait. Approaching fast. The echo back told him nothing new. But what was that strange sound blended with the ship's diesel?

Raza moved from the shelter of the back eddy and spy-hopped. A cruise ship, pinpricked with light like some luminous creature of the deepest ocean, was bearing down on him. Music was throbbing from the upper deck, filling each wave crest and shivering across his back. It drew him on and on.

"Squee, whee...wait for me. I'm coming, I'm coming too."

"Don't follow, Raza. We shall never understand their ways."

Was it the old ones trying to warn him? They were far away now, out of sound range. No use listening. Even the familiar echo in his head was fading.

"Turn, Raza. Turn before it is too late."

"Too late, too late already."

Now he was leaping and diving in the ship's wake, swimming with all his strength. The music from above surrounded him, drowning out all thoughts of his old pod.

"Farewell Raza...farewell."

When early morning came the music ended and Raza dropped back, too exhausted to continue. A lighthouse on a nearby island winked its eye at him as the ship disappeared over the horizon. "Gone," it seemed to say. "Gone."

"I know it's gone. Don't keep saying the same old thing every time you turn."

Nearby, a flock of sea scoters crooned their adrift-at-sea song,

> Home, home,
> far away from home.
> The wash of the wave,
> the turn of the tide,
> Home, home,
> far away from home.

Raza rested off the lighthouse. Snooze at the surface, slowly sink, rise again and take a breath. Over and over until he felt his strength returning.

Soon it would be day and what then? Take a good look around you, seaweed-brain. Human signs, everywhere! Thick as herring swimming in a ball. Head north again.

"Don't return to look for us here," the old bull's voice echoed.

"South...all right, I'll go south, and from there into the great, western sea."

But what were the old ones always saying, especially she who led their pod? "Choose the way carefully. Swim the southern route and you swim the way of danger."

"So what'll I do? The water here stinks of humans and it stings my skin and I don't want to stay. Squee, whee... who's there?"

Something nearby was making an awful noise.

> One, two, *tickle my toes,*
> *Three, four, frazzle my feet.*

"Can't understand what it's saying. Click...click?"
Back came the sonar picture. Bird floating on surface.
Fat, very. And funny, big feet. Too many feathers — no
good eating.

Raza dove and swam underneath the bird. There were its
feet dangling an easy snap above his head — ugly, orange,
webbed feet. Why not have some fun? He grabbed the
feet between his huge, front teeth and pulled the bird under.

"Whee, this is fun. More fun than I've had since last
summer." When Raza let go, the ball of feathers bobbed to
the surface like a styrofoam float.

"Not bad for a bird. Now watch me. This trick is called
breeching. First we speed swim, then we take off and
whee..." Where Raza touched down a fountain of spray
erupted. "Now it's your turn again."

But the bird was opening and shutting its beak and
making strange, spluttering noises. "Disreputable behaviour!
Over my defunct body will I be dragged underwater again.
I'm not a diving bird. I'm a domestic goose, Toulouse by
trade and Flora by name."

Raza carved a figure eight around the bird. "Can't
understand. Talk louder. Don't hear so well above water.
What's dis-rep-ut-able, de-funct?"

"If you don't stop running around in circles and spouting
from your brain, how can you ever hope to understand?"

"I'll stop, but not for long. Young orcas don't like staying
still. It's boring." Raza yawned, showing both sets of
gleaming teeth.

Flora back-paddled at the sight of those teeth. "I see
little point in continuing this conversation when neither
party fully understands the other."

"Squee...don't go."

"I have a sneaking suspicion that you'd like to make a meal of me, whole or in sections."

Raza squirted water through his teeth. "Me? No way. Not me."

"Then how do you explain your atrocious behaviour when we first met?" Flora ruffled the water off her feathers. "And I wish you would empty your mouth before speaking."

"Sorry." Raza spat the leftover water out. "I was having fun, that's all. We orcas like fooling around. Once my pod played with a sea lion all morning."

"Before making a meal of him, am I correct?"

"How'd you know?"

"It wasn't difficult to figure out. Your breath reeks of fish, among other things."

Raza rolled over and smacked his flipper on the surface. "Ate a salmon last night. Nothing since. Fish are the easiest to catch when you're all alone."

"And if one day fish are scarce and a plump sea bird should happen along, what then?"

"Snap, crunch, swallow...I guess."

"So how's your appetite this morning?"

"Whee...hungry as a wolf eel."

Flora shut her eyes and paddled faster. "It's been a frightfully interesting experience meeting a young orca, but I must be on my way. I'm leaving my island home — fleeing for my life you might say."

"Me tooo..." Raza whistled, catching up to the grey goose with a slight wiggle of his tail flukes.

"Wh-what an unfortunate coincidence," Flora stammered.

"Click...don't understand." Raza brought his huge head on a level with the grey goose until their eyes met. "Swim for your life, Raza. That's what old bull told me. So here I am and there you are, right? Let's swim together."

"How can I be positive that one melancholy day you won't develop an insatiable appetite for plump, domestic goose?"

"Too many big words. Head's tired now."

Raza lay motionless, with both eyes squeezed shut, letting the sounds pour in from all sides. Waves washing rocks. Sea gulls splitting clam shells. Drop and crack! Shell drift down, down...past kelp fronds, waving, slippery, past starfish and underwater cliffs. Sandy sea floor. Still.

How to tell this bird of air and words he'd never hurt a friend? Raza searched among all the sounds he knew and felt and finally said, "Not one soft feather on your head will I hurt. You have an orca's word."

"A very young orca," Flora reminded him gently. "How long can a juvenile orca remember, when he can't stay still for more than one minute?"

"This long." Raza stretched and strained with all his muscles. "Long enough yet?"

"Stop, that's quite enough! You might injure yourself permanently. I believe you."

Raza dove and surfaced with a salmon between his teeth. "Head or tail?"

"Neither, thank you very much. I'm a grass eater by design and preference."

"Mmm...too bad." The fish disappeared between his knife-sharp chompers.

"Actually I feel fortunate because grass stays put and when snow or ice covers the ground all I require is a handful of grain."

Raza sluiced a mouthful of water through his teeth to remove the bits and pieces of fish. "Fun...the chase is fun."

"We eat what we must and that's that," Flora declared. "Personally, I'd rather not dwell on the subject."

A sea gull skimming low over the water turned and circled when he spotted them. "What's up? What's this I'm seeing, a killer whale and a goose swimming together? Oh boy, wait till I tell the others."

Raza snapped at the gull. "Shut your big beak. I swim with anyone I like."

"Wait till the sun cracks through the mist. You'll be in trouble then...and don't say I didn't warn you. Oh boy, I can hardly wait to tell everybody else."

The gull flew off, squawking the news.

"Perhaps from his vantage point in the skies he sees something we don't," Flora suggested.

"Squee...not him. Watch out you big-beaked, garbage gobbler. I'll get you." Raza chased the gull to the nearest rocky island before giving up and turning around.

"Click, what's that? Boats...outboards heading our way. I've barged smack onto their fishing grounds. Old bull would kill me."

"Don't waste precious time worrying about him," Flora warned. "Dive, disappear, before the sun dissolves the mist and leaves you unprotected."

But one of the boats had already spotted Raza's dorsal fin. "Killer over there!"

"Squee...too late. Too late."

"Killer!" The voice shook the mist. "The brute has broken my line. I'll go after him."

Raza's dorsal fin trembled. "What'll I do? Where'll I go? They followed me underwater before. Trapped."

"Nonsense," Flora honked, "nonsense. Deep dive, that's what your old bull would do."

"Raza." The familiar sound skipped over the waves. "Think like an orca. Act like an orca."

The voice of his pod, wherever they were. "Right, I'll dive. But not too deep. Honk if there's trouble."

"Trouble? Certainly, certainly not. Humans are accustomed to geese. They won't bother a plain, domestic goose out for a swim."

"Who knows humans, who knows?" And Raza was gone, leaving only a line of bubbles and a circle on the surface to show where he had dived.

Boats everywhere! And one of them revving its engine and charging towards the grey goose. Click, click...goose and boat on collision course. Goose diving, floundering, too many feathers.

"Coming. I'm coming." Raza snatched the goose's feet and pulled her under. Overhead the propeller blades churned and spat the water into waves. Too loud, too dangerous, too close. He should deep dive. Disappear. Never come back. But the goose, what about the goose? He couldn't let go and he couldn't drag her deeper. Like a limp jelly fish she swung from his teeth, her feathers floating every which way. Was she dying? Don't know birds, except to eat. What'll I do?

"Squee...can you hear me now?"

As the grey goose opened her beak, bubbles of air escaped. Raza heard the bubbles smack the surface. Her air was gone — same as when he stayed underwater too long. She needed air NOW!

"Click, click?" Humans all gone. And boat sounds fading like breakers on a beach after the storm. Raza opened his mouth and the grey goose shot to the top.

"What a water-logged experience," Flora spluttered, flapping her wings and scooting around the surface. "I'm thankful to be alive. It's miraculous how you operate underwater."

"Simple as swallowing a fish," Raza squeaked. "I'll show you sometime. Whee...watch out boats or I'll bash you head-on." As he was speed swimming around the goose, the sun burst from the mist and touched his back.

"Careful," Flora warned, "with the sun reflecting off your back like a gigantic mirror they'll notice you for sure. If I were you I'd simmer down and swim away to safer places and happier days."

Raza waggled his dorsal fin. "Safer places, happier days? I like your sound. I'm catching on slowly. It's different, but I like it."

"What swims together, learns together, or so my humans used to say. Perhaps one day I shall be able to understand your underwater trills and trolls."

"Right, we're off to safer places. And I know just the spot — cove, stream, a few bay ducks."

Flora perked up. "You mentioned a stream...might there be green grass and flowers beside this stream?"

"Don't ask me. The old ones remember everything. Not me. Too long ago."

And together they followed the shoreline of the island north by northeast, dodging rocks and shoals and lying low when boats came close. As evening touched the water around them, mist began to re-form.

"Click, click...next cove, better be. Too slow. Any oyster could swim faster."

"You aren't accustomed to travelling with a Toulouse goose. We've never been noted for our speed swimming or our flying, though at singing we excel."

Raza gritted his teeth. "And too many big words."

"If you find me so utterly, utterly tiresome, you're perfectly free to go ahead."

"We swim together, remember? Around this next point and...what the?" Raza shuddered to a stop.

Smoke was curling from a small cedar cabin tucked into the cove and two humans were racing along the beach.

"Squee...bad mistake. Hope they haven't seen us.

Reverse course."

"Having seen that delectable spread of meadow, I'm not swimming one cove further," Flora protested. "Besides, it's only a boy and a small girl and they are too busy running to bother us. Haven't you noticed that most humans have single-track minds?"

"Whatever they have it's dangerous," Raza spluttered. "But I'll stop if you want. I need a fish or something to tickle my belly."

"And while you are busy fishing I shall waddle over and pay my respects to the two youngsters."

"What?" Raza almost leaped clear of the water. "Don't understand."

"I want to meet the two young ones and investigate the situation. We geese like to know what's going on, here there and everywhere."

Raza waggled both flippers. "Don't go. Too dangerous. Humans are worse than wolf eels. A scummy, scrappy lot."

"The young ones here are harmless — I can feel it in my feathers. Besides, I'm a domestic goose and in some unaccountable way I miss the company of humans."

"Squee...you do? You like them better. You don't want to swim with me anymore. I'm leaving then. Going, going, almost gone."

Flora ruffled her feathers. "Don't be foolish. I'd rather swim with you than anyone else. You rescued me from that boat, remember?"

Raza stopped and patted himself with one flipper. "Right. Good job that."

"But you must understand I yearn for humans in a different way. I was brought up in an incubator and the first sound I heard, other than the gentle hum of the machine that kept me warm, was a human voice. And when I pecked a hole through my eggshell after the necessary thirty days had passed, the first thing I saw was a human. I followed, peeping after him until..."

"Stop!" Raza clamped his gleaming teeth together. "Take care. Because if anything bad happens I'll swallow those two minnows whole."

Then he arched his back and dove to the bottom of the cove.

Jesse's Story

"Jesse, run slow." His sister's voice wailed after him. "Jesse, stop...pul-eese."

Merle's voice stuck between his shoulder blades, slowing him to a trot. In a few minutes she would catch up and grab his arm. He wanted to be alone. He needed a quiet time to think about the letter his dad had handed him before leaving for work.

"It's from your mother in Vancouver, Jesse. One of the fellows I work with brought our mail from the village."

Jesse had read the letter three times that day, but always Merle was tugging at his elbow, wheedling herself between him and the paper.

"Tell Merle, Jesse."

If she was a normal kid he'd have shouted, "Quit bugging me while I'm reading."

But Merle was not normal and maybe she never would be. Sometimes people called her dumb or retard right in front of her face. What if she understood in a different way? Thinking about that word "retard" made Jesse's fists tighten up.

"Don't you listen to their talk, Merle," he always said. "Remember I'm looking after you, no matter what."

Jesse stopped at their special sitting place, a flat rock that jutted into the water. Merle flung herself down on her stomach, like a wild animal with its tongue lolling out. A pool of spit gathered under her tongue.

Jesse closed his eyes and waited. "I'll read the letter when you stop panting, Merle. See? I've got the letter in my hand." He crinkled the paper into a rustling sound to catch her attention.

Merle sat up straight. "Letter in hand," she repeated, waving her arms in a circle.

"Merle, I can't see properly when you're waving your arms in my face. Don't you want me to read the letter from Mom now?"

"Mom now, Jesse. Mom now."

Jesse unfolded the letter and smoothed it out on the flat rock. Reading her handwriting was hard enough without all the wrinkles in the paper.

Dear Norm, Jesse and Merle,

It's been a week since I arrived here in Vancouver. Please try and understand why I suddenly up and left you three without saying a word. I know it was awful to leave while you were away fishing, but it was easier for me that way. You found my note on the table? I couldn't take another stormy fall and winter on the island. Last winter was the worst yet. Without a telephone, without electricity, without any close neighbours, I felt so cut off from the world. I had to get away for a little while, both for my own and your sakes. Forgive me if you can.

I've got a job in the evenings, waitressing. Not very good pay, but at least it's a job. I'm still looking for a place to rent. If I do find something maybe Jesse and Merle can come and stay with me. Trouble is, everywhere I ask they say no kids or pets. Do they think kids will just disappear?

Yesterday, when I was at the health clinic, I asked the doctor about Merle. She thinks Merle may be autistic, whatever that means. I went and got a pile of books from the library, but I haven't had time to read them yet. Apparently there are special schools to help these kids.

Sorry for the rushed note — I have to be at work in a few minutes.

I love you all, XOXO,

Toni

P.S. Work hard at your school work, Jesse and try and look after your little sister while Norm is at work, okay?

Jesse crumpled the paper into a tight wad and stuffed it in his jeans pocket. "There...I hope you listened Merle, because I'm not reading this letter again, ever. Understand?"

Merle tried to burrow her arm into his pocket and find the letter.

"Leave the letter alone, Merle. It's all crumpled up and ruined and I'm going to burn it in the woodstove."

"Burn stove, Jesse. Burn stove...stove burn."

"Quit it, Merle. Let's think about something else. We came down here to dig some clams for supper, remember? If we don't get them in the pail soon they won't have time to clean the sand out of their stomachs before we eat them.

45

You want a mouthful of grit, Merle? I sure don't."

Merle dragged her clam rake over the tide flats, following a crab trail. Clatter, clatter over the gravel, thump, bump, against the barnacle-covered boulder, swish, swish through the seaweed. Merle's rake caught a seagull feather and she forgot all about the crab.

"Look, Jesse, look."

"I know...it's beautiful, Merle. You can stick it in Dad's hat, the one with the wide brim that keeps the rain off." Jesse pulled the feather from the prongs. "What have you gotten into, Merle? Your rake is covered with tar or oil or something sticky. Now stay out of trouble and help me dig clams."

After Jesse pulled his rake over the coarse gravel, three clams were hanging from the prongs. "Littlenecks, the best kind. Pull them off, Merle and plop them into the pail."

"Plop, plop." Merle stuck her head inside the pail where the echo was loudest. "Plop, plop."

"Hurry, Merle. I've got more littlenecks."

Clams for dinner, twice in a row. If Mom was around we'd be having a stew or something else for a change. Not clams. She didn't like them and I don't either, Jesse thought.

He threw down his rake. "We've got enough, Merle. Now we leave them sitting peacefully in the pail and they'll siphon water in and out until there is no sand left in their guts. And then we eat 'em."

"Poof!" Merle wrinkled her nose.

"Too bad. They aren't my favourite dinner either."

Merle squeezed his arm and pointed to the headland that sheltered their cove from the southeast storms.

Jesse glanced at his watch. Three o'clock and still supper and school work to keep him busy. "All right, Merle, I guess we have time to go there. But we'll have to hurry."

Jesse gave her a hand up the final rock bluff and then sprawled on the grass, squinting his eyes against the brightness of sea and sky. Where did one end and the other begin?

"You can see straight to Vancouver, Merle, except it's below the horizon, even the tallest buildings."

Whenever they came up here she wanted to hear the same old story. What did she see — a drowned city with fish swimming over the rooftops and seaweed waving through open windows? Their mom was there too, her face rippled by the distant water. Perhaps in the blackest night the lights from the city could reach up and touch their sky, enough for them to see. One night he would sneak up here alone and look.

"Ouch!" Merle sat down on his upturned foot and made him look where she was pointing.

"What do you see there?" Jesse shaded his eyes. "Lots of splashing. Probably birds diving at a herring ball or something dead floating on the surface. Wish we had Dad's binoculars. You know what, Merle? It looks like a whale, only Dad said whales don't come here anymore."

Merle tugged his arm. "Whale, Jesse."

"How would you know, Merle? Dad says all the narrow passages on this side of the island made it too easy to shoot whales and now they don't like coming here."

"Whale, Jesse."

"Come on, Merle, it's time to go home. Look at the tide covering the gravel flats."

They clambered down the bluffs and followed the edge of the rock where the water hadn't reached yet. Merle ran along the tide line, kicking the foam and bubbles with her feet.

"Watch out, it might grab you, Merle."

Jesse picked up the pail and carried it to their cabin,

being careful not to slosh water over his boot tops. The cabin still felt warm from the late afternoon sun and the leftover embers of the fire. When Merle wasn't looking, Jesse threw their mom's letter into the woodstove. The ashes flickered, then flared up and caught the paper. Good…it was gone. He added more alder chunks and shoved a pot of lukewarm water over the hottest place. In no time it would be boiling and ready to cook the clams.

"Better get busy," Jesse sighed, dragging his schoolwork from a cardboard box stashed in one corner of the cabin. Why did the Correspondence Office have to send such a mountain of stuff? Just to read the directions had taken him a whole day. Jesse opened math paper number two and bent over the smudge of eraser marks. "I still don't get it," he complained, after ten minutes had ticked by.

He chewed on his pencil and stared glumly at Merle who was swishing the water around in the clam bucket. So much for leaving the clams peaceful! "You might as well toss 'em into the boiling water."

Merle shook her head. "Hot…eee, eee."

"They don't feel a thing, Merle and they don't squeak either. You're thinking of crabs or lobsters and how they turn red when they hit boiling water."

"Hot, Jesse."

"Here, give the bucket to me and I'll toss them in."

Afterwards Jesse went back to his math paper and doodled a letter to his adviser in the margin.

Dear Mr. Clayton,

This is Jesse writing from the boonies. Things are pretty rotten around here and I'm too dumb for grade seven. How about sending me back to 000000 which equals kindergarten in my great math.

Yours cluelessly, Jesse

P.S. Was Einstein a genius from the start or did he take time to develop? Is there a chance for me? Jesse again.

He drew a goose egg underneath — it was growing bigger and bigger and hatching into a monster with huge, hairy toes...

Jesse felt Merle stroking the back of his hand where the veins stood out, soft and blue. "Thanks, Merle. I wish you could help, but it's no use. I'm too dumb."

He wandered over to the window and peered out. Already it was growing too dark for working unless he turned on the Coleman lantern and he hated the noisy thing.

"Come on, Merle, we better chop the onions and potatoes and carrots into the clam water so they have time to cook together. It's getting dark and Dad will be home anytime and we still have to go dump the empty shells into the cove."

Meeting

Long before they reached the water Jesse hoisted Merle onto his shoulders so she couldn't run off and get herself soaked.

"Now you can see everything, Merle. There's only water and mist falling down with the night and lots of fish and maybe way out a boat with a light coming on and..."

Something big splashed nearby, raining drops of water through the mist. Jesse swung around, but not fast enough to see the thing, whatever it was.

Merle dug her sharp, little heels into his ribs and squealed. "Whale, Jesse...whale."

"Don't be silly, Merle. I told you whales don't come this close. It was probably a seal chasing some chum salmon into the creek."

The splash was too loud for a seal. Jesse knew that. What if it was a ghost canoe coming their way? Their cabin was sitting right on the place where people used to live years and years ago. Norm had showed him the bank where white clam shells were mixed with the fire-blackened earth. Sometimes when the mist fell down grey and close, the old people gathered by the shore again and took to their high-prowed canoes.

"I never dug too many of your clams," Jesse whispered as he dumped the bucket of empty shells into the water. "Honest. Come on, Merle, let's get back to the cabin."

But she kept spurring her sharp heels into his ribs and turning him away from the Coleman lantern that was shining like a lighthouse beacon from their cabin window. "Pul-eese, Jesse."

"We've got to hurry," Jesse pleaded. "Look, the light has come on and that means Dad is home and probably hungry as a bear. Besides my boot has a hole and the water is flooding in and I'm freezing.... There's nothing to see out there, Merle, honestly."

A loud, trumpeting noise came from the water's edge. Something was rolling across the beach towards them, but in the dim light Jesse couldn't see what and he didn't want to find out. He turned and galloped towards the cabin.

Merle slid off his back. "Birdball," she giggled, running towards the thing. "Birdball."

"You come back here, Merle." No point yelling when she was roaring off like a wild forest fire. When he finally caught up she was bending over the grey goose, stroking the soft feathers.

"It's a goose," Jesse told her as if he'd known that all along, "a tame farm goose. Wonder where it comes from?"

Merle rested her head on the goose's back and let the feathers tickle her nose.

Jesse pulled her away. "Watch out, Merle. Dad says geese will fly at you sometimes and whop you with their wings."

Merle clung to the goose's neck. "Uh, uh, Jesse."

"All right, I'll carry the goose to our cabin if you promise to follow."

Merle ran through the foam and seaweed at the water's edge, pointing and waving her arms. But Jesse wasn't in a listening or seeing mood.

"It's nothing, Merle, just the waves swooshing around the rocks." The goose was heavy and the feathers tickled his chin and made him want to sneeze.

The cabin door opened, casting a rectangle of light into the mist. "Jesse...Merle," their father called.

Would the mist sneak in and snuff out the light before they could get there? Once through the door he'd be safe. Nothing could catch him.

"Jesse, Merle, where are you?"

Merle raced ahead and stomped on the patch of light. Catching both arms, Norm swung her through the open door and landed her safely inside. "Say, Jesse," he called, "what have you got there?"

Jesse put the goose down and rubbed his arms where the feathers had been scratching. "Merle discovered her on the beach."

Norm shone his flashlight at the goose. "It's not the first time a domestic goose has been caught out in high winds and couldn't get back to shore. Was she by herself?"

"Yes."

"Uh, uh." Merle shook her head until the wool cap she was wearing fell over her eyes. "Uh, uh, Jesse." And without warning she slipped past them, racing towards the splashing sounds in the cove.

What was it? Did Norm hear, too? Jesse tried to blot out

the sounds as he plunged after his sister. Somewhere far out in the darkness he caught Merle and held her arms tight so they couldn't whack him.

"Come on, Merle. We're two grey geese waddling back to our cabin for supper. Pretend you have a hurt foot and I have to help."

Norm patted Jesse on the back when they waddled up. "Thanks, Jesse. Sometimes I think you and your mother are the only ones who can handle her."

"Don't say that, Dad. I know Merle better, that's all.... Can I give the goose some cracked wheat?" he asked, trying to change the subject.

"Sure, but only a cupful, Jesse. We need what's left for baking bread."

Jesse watched as Flora gobbled up the grain, then he shut the cabin door softly so as not to scare her. Inside it was warm, but with only three of them, the room felt empty. All week long that emptiness had been chewing inside Jesse's stomach.

"Come on," Norm called from the table. "Clam chowder is getting cold."

Jesse shoved more alder wood into the stove and stamped on the ashes that drifted to the floor, anything to delay sitting down. From a distance he watched Merle slobbering soup down her front and Norm guzzling another bottle of home brew. The flames worried around the fresh alder chunks. Finally Jesse shoved the stove door shut with one knee and went to sit down.

"That's your third bottle of beer," he complained.

Norm grinned. "Aren't I lucky to have someone keeping track for me."

Jesse shrugged his shoulders and tucked into the chowder. If he was careful he could avoid the bits of clam floating grey and listless on the surface. The only sounds in the cabin were the roar of the Coleman lantern and Merle sucking soup off her spoon.

"How would you like to go and live with your mother in the city?" Norm asked abruptly.

"I dunno," Jesse mumbled. "I haven't been there since I was a tiny baby."

"Don't you get lonely by yourself?" Norm persisted.

"There's Merle," Jesse pointed out.

"Sure, I know, but she's hardly company. It's no good your being alone all day, Jesse. We've got to figure out some better plan."

Jesse shrugged again. "Maybe I do get a bit lonely, but you're always home at night." He watched his dad open another bottle of home brew.

Suddenly Norm brought his fist down on the table. "Isn't a man entitled to a few beers after his wife has left him with two kids? And one of them crazy as a coot. Look at her!"

Merle had spilled her dish of chowder and was lapping up the bits and pieces from the table like a small puppy.

"She can't help it," Jesse shouted. "Just because she's not coordinated properly you get mad." His face was pale as he shoved the chair away from the table. "I'm not hungry for any more chowder," he added more quietly. "I'll do the dishes, okay Dad?"

"Sure, Jesse, thanks. Go ahead and do what you want. If you don't mind I'll sit here a while longer. It was a rough day in the woods. One of the other fallers, an old friend of mine, got hurt when the tree he was cutting lost a branch way up...came right down on his shoulder."

After the dishes were done, Jesse opened the cabin door to throw out the greasy water. "Merle..." She was sitting with the mist and the night and the grey goose curled in her lap. "Merle, you haven't a jacket or a hat. You'll catch cold."

Merle shook her head. "No cold, Jesse."

"Merle, you have to come inside. The goose needs some sleep too."

"Goose sleep." Merle tried to carry Flora into the cabin.

"No, Merle, the goose has to sleep outside. With all her feathers she would be too hot in the cabin."

Jesse shooed the grey goose outside and shut the door. Norm was slumped over the table sound asleep. Knowing it would be impossible to wake or move him, Jesse draped a blanket across his shoulders and stuffed the woodstove with fir logs to keep the cabin warm long into the night.

"There." Jesse wiped his sooty hands on the back of his jeans and held them over the stove for a last minute toasting.

After he turned off the Coleman lantern there was only the sound of the fire eating away at the wood and occasionally exploding a pocket of fir gum. Jesse climbed the ladder to his loft and opened his sleeping bag. From there he could keep an eagle eye on the whole cabin: Merle snuffling in the corner bunk bed, Norm hunched over the table beside an empty bottle, chinks of light from the woodstove reflecting off the log walls...

For the moment he was warm, but eventually the cold would come seeping through the foamie and into his sleeping bag. Jesse peered out the small window beside his head. The moon had burrowed a hole through the mist and was shining on the creek where the grey goose was standing. As he watched, Flora dipped her head in the water, tilted her head up and swallowed. Then she splashed water over her back and with her beak carefully preened each feather. That done, she tucked her head under one wing and rested.

It was nice knowing there was someone else out there.

Jesse's head gradually eased back onto the pillow.

"Jesse, Jesse..." It was Merle's voice breaking into his sleep. "Go pee!"

Jesse clung tighter to the warm spot in his sleeping bag, hoping Merle would forget and drop off to sleep.

But the calls became more frantic. "Jesse...come Jesse."

Why was Norm still snoring? No one could sleep through that racket. It isn't fair. He's closer. He ought to take Merle to the outhouse. Jesse dug deeper into his sleeping bag. "It's too cold for going outside, Merle. Use your pail."

"No pail," Merle wailed.

Jesse squirmed from his bag. If he didn't hurry Merle might flood the bunk bed and then he'd spend half the morning ripping the thing apart and washing sheets in the icy creek water. Too much bother to heat the water. "No wonder Mom ran away," he grumbled. "One day maybe I'll be gone too and nobody will know where to look because I won't leave a note."

He hated Norm's snoring. "Pig!" he whispered under his breath as he slipped past the sleeping body.

Merle was dancing around on one foot now. "Pul-eese, Jesse."

He opened the door and felt the rush of cold air. "Okay, Merle, I'll wait here by the door while you run to the outhouse. No...you go by yourself. And be quick!"

Jesse stared out at the cove. Some glistening object floating on the surface caught his attention — a raft of seaweed, driftwood, a styrofoam float perhaps? It seemed too big. Besides, it was moving fast now, swimming towards shore. And going to meet it was the grey goose. A sound, almost too high for him to hear, a sound like high-pitched singing or whistling, vibrated through the night air.

Merle came racing around the corner of the cabin. "Was

that you? Did you make that noise, Merle?"

She danced around him, flapping her wrists. "Uh, uh, Jesse. Uh, uh."

"Quit it, Merle. I want to go back inside."

He tried to catch her, but she ran towards the cove. Then cupping both hands around her mouth she blew a sound that was at once all sounds and no sound.

Shivers ran down Jesse's neck. Was he imagining things? Had he heard the song of the great ocean, the song of underwater rivers and currents too huge to measure, the song of beasts moving through the darkness, the song of drowned cities, of winds and tides and storms...

Whumpf! Raza surfaced and blew a jet of air and water from his blowhole. The echo bounced back and forth between the rocky headlands.

With the moon shining down there was no mistaking what was out there. Jesse stared at the whale and back to his sister. "You knew it was there all along, didn't you Merle? And you even sang a song to the whale."

"Sangsong." Merle giggled, whirling around with the sound of the words. "Songsang, sangsong."

Jesse picked her up from the damp grass. "It's got to be a killer whale," he told her. "No other whale, except maybe a grey, would come in this close. I hope it doesn't eat our goose. Killers eat everything you know — fish, birds, seals, sea lions, even other whales. Dad wouldn't want him hanging around in our cove because he'll eat all our fish and we won't catch any more cod or snapper for breakfast. Too bad, eh Merle?"

Merle squeezed her eyes shut and made a funny clicking sound with her tongue. "Clack, clack..." The echo ran along the rocky edges of the cove.

As Jesse watched, the whale rose above the surface,

swivelling his huge head around until he was facing them.

"Clack, clack..."

"Quit it, Merle. You're supposed to talk, not make funny noises. Remember, you aren't a little baby anymore, you're almost to my shoulder."

Raza rolled over, smacked his flippers on the water, then slowly submerged.

Merle squealed and struggled against Jesse's grip.

"It's only a whale and it will be here tomorrow."

"Morrow...morrow..." Merle stomped her bare feet on the grass.

"I don't know about you, Merle, but I'm freezing. Let's go inside."

Jesse banged the door shut and rattled the ladder leading to his loft. Too bad if it woke Norm. Now he was wide awake and it would take ages to fall asleep because the warm spot in his sleeping bag had gone and even if he did manage to fall asleep it wouldn't do any good because he would wake up bad tempered and stay that way all day. Jesse rolled himself into a tight ball around his feet. In a couple more hours, at quarter to six exactly, he would get up and light the woodstove and put on water for porridge. At seven exactly, his Dad would walk the kilometer out to the main road where the rest of the logging crew always picked him up. And then he, Jesse, would have the day to himself until Norm got home around five. Same old thing, day after day after day.... And no Mom around to laugh at some dumb joke, or worry about the hole in his jeans, or bake a bunch of chocolate chip cookies, or nag about correspondence courses. Thinking about that math paper made him feel tired. Stuck in the middle with nobody around to help...

Jesse scratched his feet against the sleeping bag. Gradually they were thawing out. Maybe he could manage to drift off to sleep. And who said tomorrow had to be more of the same old thing? If the weather held, maybe they could take the boat out for a spin and find that whale.

Jesse could hear his father's voice warning, "I don't mind you fooling around in the cove, but don't take our outboard into the main passage, Jesse. Tides are too unpredictable out there and the surges can easily swamp a small boat. You wouldn't last five minutes in that cold water. One of these weekends when I've got time you and I will take the boat up one of the big mainland inlets. How's that?"

Jesse snuggled down in his sleeping bag and pulled the edges tight around his neck. Now that was something to dream about — inlets as long as any Norwegian fiord, huge cliffs, waterfalls you could sneak behind in the boat, snow covered mountains, glaciers coming down almost to the sea... Maybe sometime they could bushwhack up to where the rivers roar from the great ice caves. Norm had been there once. And they could walk on the ice and climb a peak and look down on the world like an eagle does. And what was on the other side of those shining mountains?

Jesse gave a little jump as he fell off to sleep. What about Merle? Would she come too?

Travellers Together

"Greetings and a good evening," Flora honked across the chilly waters of the cove. "I can't begin to tell you how splendid it was walking on dry land and eating green grass again."

"Then don't." Raza huffed a jet of steam into the night air. "Too long. How come it took so long? I could have eaten a cove full of fish in that time."

"If I may remind you it wasn't a question of eating a million fish like some bloodthirsty creatures I know do."

Raza sank low in the water. "Too long. I was lonely. Are you going again?"

Flora swam closer and peered into his half opened eye. "Cheer up. I'm still here, aren't I?"

"Squee...not for long. You like them better."

61

"What nonsense," Flora honked. "Utterly. Now would you like to hear what I learned about the human youngsters?"

"Maybe..."

"You can't find better investigators than we geese. Stop, look, listen, follow up the story and honk for all it's worth."

"Go on then...the youngsters?"

"I have discovered that they are alone most of the time and liable to land themselves in trouble — serious trouble."

"So...I'm alone, you're alone. Where's your mother or father?"

"You've stumped me there," Flora admitted, "but it's not the same for us. What we know and do, the very young of humans have to be taught — swimming, waddling, everything. With their lack of instinct you might even call them clueless."

"Whee...what's lack of instinct?"

"No ears, eyes, nose for danger."

"None?" Raza dove under the goose and surfaced on the other side.

"Barely a smattering."

"Too dangerous," he whistled. "Let's not get mixed up with them."

"We can hardly avoid becoming mixed up with them," Flora pointed out. "We are all in the same cove and unless we feel like moving on..."

"Not now," Raza groaned. "I'm stiff and hurting all over."

"Then stay still and I'll tell you everything I know about the human youngsters."

"All right. But not too long-winded. I'm feeling sleepy." Raza yawned until his full set of chompers gleamed silver in the moonlight.

"There they are now," Flora honked softly, "standing outside the cabin with the moon shining on their faces.

What mysterious creatures they are!"

Raza trembled. "Listen, I hear her singing. I think she knows all about us."

"Oh, she is perceptive all right. I could feel that while she was stroking my head."

"You... you let them touch your head?" Raza swallowed a mouthful of salt water by mistake.

"I'd forgotten how delicious it felt," Flora said dreamily.

"Dangerous and dumb. Boring, too. I'm going back to sleep now."

"Don't be foolish," Flora scolded. "Although an outsider might doubt it, I will always be your true friend."

"Positive?" The whale opened one eye and lowered himself until he was staring into the grey goose's eye.

"Of course. How could I ever forget the valiant actions of the one who saved my life?"

"I can stay awake," Raza whistled. "Start with the boy."

"Well, he's twelve years old or thereabouts — the same age as another acquaintance of mine, in a different cove, not so very long ago..."

"Yes, go on, go on!"

"I heard his name — it's Jesse."

"Nice, a nice sound."

"He is smallish for his age, with freckles over his nose and a mess of curly hair. What else do you want to know?" Flora asked.

"The important part." Raza smacked his tail flukes on the water. "What's this boy, this Jesse, like?"

"Patient, steadfast and stout of heart. But he feels all alone in the cove and this frightens him."

"I understand the boy," Raza squeaked. "Now, the girl."

"Everything about her is a mystery, except for the long, dark hair that falls across her face. When she leaned over, it brushed against my feathers. I know her name is Merle, but what I don't know almost scares me. She is like no other human I have ever met."

"Does she know what we creatures know?" Raza asked, after circling three times around the grey goose.

"Who knows? With her anything is possible."

For a long time nothing stirred under the silent moon as the tide rocked the whale and the goose towards shore...

Inside the cabin Norm's alarm went off and eventually crawled to a stop.

Jesse stirred. Quarter to six, but it felt way earlier. He waited a few more minutes, hoping somebody would move. No luck! If Mom was home, she'd have the stove going by now and a kettle of fresh creek water warming and maybe some huckleberry or blackberry muffins in the oven. No use dreaming.

Jesse forced himself out of the sleeping bag and into his jeans and sweater. Darn, another hole in one sock where the gumboot rubbed the heel. After splashing some ice water on his face, Jesse went to wake Norm. Sometime during the night he had moved into bed.

"Dad, it's five to six. Time to get up."

"Uh, thanks Jesse. Must have slept right through the alarm... and sorry about last night. I wasn't very helpful if I remember."

"That's okay, Dad. There weren't many dishes to wash up."

"I wasn't thinking only of the dishes, Jesse. It's asking a lot of you to stay here by yourself, day after day. But at least I've got work on the island here and can come home at night. Most of the fallers I know have headed upcoast or wherever there's any decent timber left. You stick to your correspondence courses, Jesse, and go into some other work — that's good advice from an old faller."

"You're not old, Dad."

"I feel old, Jesse. Most of the fellows in our logging show are half my age. Like the old song says, if a tree don't kill you, then the back pain will."

Jesse crumpled up a sheet of newspaper and stuffed it into the firebox. With his hatchet he split some cedar strips off a large chunk standing beside the stove and in no time flames were crackling the kindling.

At the first pop of the cedar wood Merle opened her eyes and sniffed. Like a deer or some other wild animal, Jesse thought. It was the same every morning — she didn't say a word — just lay there sniffing and listening.

"We're out of newspaper," Jesse announced.

"We're out of almost everything," Norm said. "How about a trip into town this weekend, Jesse? We'll take the Saturday off, catch an early ferry over, shop all afternoon, eat a pizza, take in the early show and be home before midnight."

"Sounds great, Dad, but what about Merle? You know how it is when she gets tired."

But did Norm really know? He wasn't there the day Merle took off and jumped into the water near the ferry landing. While his mom disappeared to hunt up some dry clothes, he had to keep an eye on Merle. She just sat there splashing water like a sea gull, ignoring the crowd. And to make everything worse, an older guy he knew came strolling by...

"You actually live with that crazy kid, Jesse?"

He didn't know whether to laugh the remark off, fight the guy, or what. Maybe it sounded funny telling Norm later on...

"Don't you worry about your sister, Jesse. If I can handle a chainsaw and a falling tree and the worst weather on the coast, I can easily handle her. Any problems and I'll carry her back. Watch this."

With one hand Norm snatched Merle from the bunk bed and lifted her over his head. Merle's eyes and mouth opened wide in a scream.

"Dad, don't! It scares her when you do things too quickly and out of their usual order."

Norm set her down cautiously as if she were a piece of old china about to fly apart.

Merle stretched out her arms to Jesse and for a few moments he held her near the woodstove. "More pop-sticks, Jesse."

He shoved in another cedar piece. "That's the last of the noisy ones, Merle, the rest are alder."

She crouched beside the stove, listening.

"How about some pancakes?" Norm asked. "I found some ready mix in the cupboard and if we make 'em on top of the stove it will save washing up."

But the back of the stove was too hot, the front was too cool, the batter stuck, it slipped between the cracks, it flowed away — nothing seemed to work. The pancakes were a disaster.

"Better luck next time," Norm remarked, trying to crack a joke. A splotch of batter had caught in his hair.

"Mom...Mom." Jesse tried not to think about her or the yummy huckleberry pancakes she always made.

It was almost time for Norm to leave. Jesse watched as he poured the leftover coffee into a thermos, pulled on his heavy wool pants and sweater and stowed his hard hat and the rest of the faller's gear in a packsack.

"Guess I'm about ready, Jesse. Can you see anything I've forgotten?"

Jesse handed him a paper bag. "Don't forget the sandwiches I made, Dad."

"Peanut butter and jam?"

"Yep, we're out of tinned meat and I gave you the last hunk of cheese day before yesterday."

"Bye, Jesse." Norm squashed him in a gigantic bear hug. "If you've got time this afternoon you could buck up the rest of that fallen maple. But use the smaller chainsaw while I'm away and be extra careful, eh?"

Jesse eyed his Dad. He looked good in his work clothes, as tough and weather-beaten as the woods he worked in. Nothing could possibly hurt his dad.

"See you later," Jesse called out as he watched Norm disappear down the old skid road.

"Later, later." Merle waved too.

Except for the humming of the kettle on the stove it was suddenly very quiet. Too quiet, Jesse thought. He peered through the window for some signs of life. The grey goose was floating near shore, but the whale was nowhere to be seen. Had he dreamed that gigantic creature under the silver moon? Jesse blew on the window pane until it was misty, then traced the outline of a whale and poked a circle for an eye.

Merle made squiggle-marks around the whale.

"Don't smudge my picture off," Jesse complained.

But she was only adding songs for the whale to sing.

Jesse stared through the whale's eye. "Look at the weather out there, Merle. Who wants to stay inside and do correspondence? Not me." Jesse tossed his books back into the box. "Come on, Merle. Get your boots and let's go."

Outside the sun had broken through the mist and the whole world was steaming with the warmth — the walls of the cabin, the creek, the meadow leading down to the cove, their favourite sitting rock, even the sea itself was on fire.

"Smoke," Merle cried, trying to curl her tongue around the steam.

When Jesse tried to pull her off the damp grass she only tightened up like a clam and burrowed deeper.

"I know what," he suggested. "Let's take our boat and have a close-up look at that whale. And if the channel is calm enough we'll run over to the Shelter Bay store for some ice cream. Wouldn't that be fun, Merle? Sitting in the boat and eating ice cream."

"Icing cream," Merle repeated after him.

Would Norm ever be furious if he discovered they had taken the boat to Shelter Bay! But what he doesn't know won't bother him, Jesse reasoned, and in good weather there was zero danger. Hadn't he been there with Dad hundreds of times? Still, he couldn't blot out the sound of Norm's voice and the warning, "Don't go into the channel alone, Jesse. Winds and tides are too unpredictable."

"Better wear your warmest jacket, Merle. Even with the sun shining it will be cold on the water this time of year." Jesse's hands were shaking, but not from the cold.

Before leaving the cabin Jesse double-checked the tide timetable. The low low, or the lowest tide of the whole twenty-four hour cycle was at night — he knew that already. But what he needed to find out was the difference between tides during the daylight hours. If it was too great he wouldn't dare run their little outboard against the current. Jesse ran his finger down the long columns of figures; time of day in one, height of tide in the other... just as he thought, the tide was up all day with less than a meter difference between the high low and low high. No problem.

Jesse dropped the timetable into his packsack, along with Norm's navigation chart, flashlight and extra sweaters. "Can you think of anything else, Merle?"

She pulled two spoons from the drawer and waved them in his face. "Spoons, Jesse."

"Good for you, Merle. Spoons for the ice cream. I'd forgotten."

Outside the cabin they gulped down the fresh air like a couple of fishes poking their heads above water. It smelled of cedar, fir and hemlock, mixed with wood smoke and salt and brewed by the sun. Before Jesse could grab Merle's hand, she escaped to the beach, crackling her boots over the skeleton oyster and clam shells.

"Come back here, Merle. If you get all wet we can't go."

As she stooped to pick up a stone shining beneath the water, a wave rippled in and caught her hair. The grey goose and the whale swam closer.

Jesse caught her arm. "What did I say about the water, Merle? Now hold my hand and don't let go."

Their boat was tied to a floating dock made of several cedar logs strapped together. The logs were always wet and slippery and Merle was always falling off.

"Go sit in the bow, Merle, and don't forget to fasten your life jacket." Norm made them wear life jackets, even for short trips. Crazy not to in these waters, he said.

Before shoving off Jesse checked the gear stashed under the orange tarp — spare engine, gas can, extra life jacket, first aid kit, tools.... Good for Norm. Maybe his pancake breakfasts weren't the greatest, but he sure knew his way around the outdoors. Jesse pushed with one oar, letting the boat glide forward with the momentum.

Whoosh! The noise of the whale surfacing nearby startled Jesse. Why was it so close?

"Merle, get back," he shouted. Stupid little kid! She was hanging right over the whale's open mouth. And take a look at those teeth.

"Sit down," he yelled again.

The whale sank and lay like a dark shadow beneath the surface.

"He's lurking somewhere. There he is, over there. I see him. Don't move from that seat, Merle."

Her eyes flashed. "Bad, bad...Jesse." She curled herself into a caterpillar ball and wouldn't look up.

"I won't start the engine while you are sulking."

Merle relaxed the caterpillar coils, but she still kept the prickles.

"Killer whales can be very dangerous," Jesse explained, pronouncing each word carefully, to make sure she understood. "If you fall in the water he might swallow you."

Merle shook her head.

"Well, didn't you see his teeth? Way longer than your longest finger, Merle. And if you lean over once more, I'm not taking you in the boat. Get it?"

Merle's head kept swinging.

She's going into one of her fits, Jesse thought. And there is nobody around to help me. What if she can't or won't come back? Maybe the noise of the engine will bring her back....Jesse swung his whole weight into pulling the starting cord.

When Merle heard the roar of the engine she stopped shaking her head.

"Hi Merle." Jesse called and waved his hand, but she was still staring back to where the whale and the grey goose were floating...

"Humans!" Raza whooshed. "I've had enough of them."

"You do have an impressive set of gnashers," Flora pointed out. "People can easily get the wrong idea."

"Wrong everything," Raza whistled. "Have you seen the stuff they toss in our ocean?"

70

"Some of my best friends are humans," Flora said. "They are as different from one another as you and I."

"Whuumph... didn't answer my question."

"So with no virtues whatsoever, how do you suppose humans became the lords of all creation?"

Raza smacked his tail flukes on the water. "Don't ask me. Maybe air is easier than water. Humans... sick of 'em."

"Even if what you say about humans is true, surely these youngsters aren't guilty? I say we ought to follow their boat in case they run into some unforeseen trouble."

"So? None of my business. None of yours."

"How utterly, utterly juvenile can you get!" Flora honked. "Everything is everybody's business nowadays or we are in for big, bad trouble. At least we geese don't ignore the problems. See you later when you grow up."

Raza watched with one open eye as the grey goose paddled after the boat. "Goodbye feather-brain... blubber belly."

The goose ignored him.

"Squee, whee... you'll never catch up."

Stupid goose wouldn't listen to him.

"Dangerous, hunters everywhere. Watch out."

Still the goose swam on.

Raza started to swim after her, slowly at first, then gradually accelerating to top speed. With each sweeping motion of his tail flukes the pain from his wounds grew worse. What had those humans done?

"Coming, I'm coming tooo..." Raza dove and surfaced with the grey goose on his back. "Ought to let you sink or swim," he wheezed, trying to sound like old bull.

Not far ahead of them the boat edged around the point and into the main channel. Although the tide was running slack, Jesse could feel the prow of their boat tossing about like a spirited horse. He braced himself and eased down on the throttle. After a while he didn't even notice the water boiling and bursting against the side of the boat.

Merle was still staring back at the cove. When Jesse glanced around he could have sworn he saw a flash of black and white. Was that whale following them?

A tug came down the centre of the channel, pulling a logboom. Long before he actually saw the logs, Jesse caught the tangy smell of yellow cedar. He swung their boat towards the opposite shore, well away from the big tug's path. As the current hit them broadside on, Jesse noticed that the trees on shore were moving in the wrong direction.

"Going backwards," he muttered. "Current's too strong for our boat. Have to keep her pointing upstream. But watch it, eh? Stay clear of the wash. Those big diesels really churn the water."

Whew! They were making headway again and the trees were moving in the right direction. Jesse's grip on the engine relaxed. Already the boom was past them and Shelter Bay lay around the next headland.

School

As the boat scraped the dock, Jesse jumped out and tied the stern rope to a metal ring. "Throw me the bow rope, Merle."

Instead, she wound the rope around her arm and started thumping it against the dock.

"What about the ice cream, Merle? And have you forgotten the generator?" Whenever they came with Norm she always rushed behind the store where the diesel generator roared and spat out its black exhaust smoke. "But first you have to hand me the rope, Merle."

She stretched out her arm while Jesse unwound the coils.

"Are you new kids?" A boy was watching them from

the ramp which led onto the dock. "Neat landing you just made."

"Thanks," Jesse mumbled. "It happens sometimes." Who was this guy? And what did he mean calling them new kids?

"You should see the bashes on our boat. Dad calls me Captain Crunch, otherwise known as Woody." He waited while Jesse tied the other rope. "Where you from?"

"Across the channel."

"Boy, you're lucky. Wish I could come by myself, but my dad makes me take the dumb water taxi."

"Yeah," Jesse agreed. Good thing Norm wasn't listening in. Would this kid ever stop talking?

Woody consulted his watch. "Ten minutes walk up the hill, minus four minutes till school starts, makes trouble. We better start hiking."

So that's what he'd meant by new kids. "I'm not going to school," Jesse started to say, but the words fizzled out. Why can't I? How come Norm never told me about this school? I hate correspondence courses. I hate being alone all day. And as long as Norm doesn't find out...

"Hey, you coming?" Woody shouted from the ramp.

"Uh... sure." The words petered out again. Please, please, Merle, don't go into a temper tantrum and ruin everything.

"Listen," Jesse whispered to her, "we're going to school today, a real school with other kids and a teacher. It will be way more fun than the pretend one all by ourselves."

Miracle — no fuss! After turning back to wave at something, she followed them up the old skid road that led to school. Away from the water it grew steadily hotter. Ten minutes walk? "More like half an hour," Jesse grumbled. If they could only stop to strip away their jackets and sweaters, but Woody kept hurrying them along.

Jesse stooped to yank off a trailing blackberry vine that had wrapped itself around his ankle. Now where had Woody disappeared to? "Hurry, Merle. We've lost him somewhere."

A few seconds later Woody sprang from behind a highway stop sign that some joker had stuck beside the road. "You know what? I've forgotten your names already."

"I never told you our names," Jesse muttered crossly, wiping off the sweat stinging his eyes.

"So I didn't forget — great!" Woody flapped the pages of the book he was carrying. "I'm always forgetting. It drives Mr. George crazy. He's our teacher in case I didn't tell you."

Maybe he'll quit talking if I tell him our names, Jesse figured. "I'm Jesse, if you really want to know. And Merle's my sister."

"Not much of a talker is she? Wish my twin sister was half as quiet. She's always yakking at me about something."

Merle stopped listening to the daisy she had picked and watched Woody from behind her outstretched hands.

"She has trouble talking," Jesse explained.

"You mean she has something wrong with her, a few parts missing?"

"I dunno exactly, but she hears everything — spiders spinning their webs, deer springing over moss, a worm burrowing underground, a flower nodding its head..."

"No kidding! Do you think she'll turn into a detective or a teacher or something like that?"

Jesse shook his head. "I doubt it. She has too many other troubles."

Merle was still staring at Woody from the crack she'd made between her little fingers. As he tried to bound off, she caught his hand and giggled.

Jesse couldn't believe his eyes. Merle, who hid from

people, who never looked anyone straight in the face, was actually holding a stranger's hand.

Woody grinned. "At least somebody thinks I'm great." He waved ahead to a clearing in the trees. "There's our school. Ten minutes late. We sure didn't beat any speed records getting here."

"I thought it would be bigger," Jesse said, eying the two-story cedar building.

"Yeah? Well, it's a wonder we ever finished. Never build anything with parents. It was nonstop nag all summer. No fooling around on the roof you kids, watch that hammer, leave the wet cement alone, will you quit yakking and work!"

A goat, munching on a lilac bush beside the front door, lifted its head and gave them a bored look.

"He does the lawn work," Woody explained, "cutting, pruning, fertilizing, you name it — he does it. Except the kids have to shovel up the pellets he drops everywhere and come spring we plant flowers and veggies in the stuff."

Jesse couldn't concentrate on a word Woody was saying. There was still time to escape. Something was bound to go wrong. Merle would have a temper tantrum, he'd flub his story (the story he hadn't invented yet), the teacher would insist on talking to Norm...a hundred things could go wrong.

"Didn't hear what I was saying, eh? Look, don't worry. There are only fifteen of us here, sixteen counting Mr. George. And if a southeaster is blowing up half the kids can't come. Besides, the islanders here are pretty friendly." Woody screwed his eyes and mouth into a fierce scowl.

Jesse braced himself for Merle's scream, but she only giggled and made a face back. Before he had time to protest, Woody was shoving them through the open door.

"Find an empty, wooden peg for your jackets and leave

your boots downstairs, okay?"

Jesse gripped Merle's hand as he felt himself being propelled up the stairs.

"Two new students for you, Mr. George," he heard Woody saying. "Jesse and Merle. I dunno... found them hanging around the dock. They didn't know the way here, so I stayed behind.... And thanks for not counting me late again, Mr. George."

From far away Jesse heard their two names being called. He squeezed Merle's hand more tightly. We shouldn't have come. Why did I let Woody bring us here? I've forgotten what I was going to say. He felt Merle's fingers pulling away, but he couldn't move or even glance up. It was like a bad dream suffocating him, turning his muscles into mush.

A hand came down on his shoulder. The force made his body, the room, the whole building shake. "Well, Jesse," Mr. George was saying, "we're pleased to have you with us, even though you are starting late. You've been taking correspondence courses I guess?"

Jesse tried to swallow whatever was blocking his throat, but it wouldn't budge. It was years since he had been in a real school. He was used to being all alone or with Merle... and where was she anyhow?

Mr. George pointed to an alcove off the main room where Merle was stretched out listening to a tape recorder. "She seems to feel right at home with us."

"Merle!" The sound burst inside his head like the sun streaming through the skylight above her.

"Don't worry, Jesse, she's all right. Now tell me about yourself."

Jesse swallowed again and took a deep breath.

"You are taking correspondence... " Mr. George tried to coax the words out.

"Yes... grade seven."

"And what about your sister?"

"She's never done any school work."

"Why is that, Jesse?"

"Because my dad has been moving around to different logging camps. And besides, Merle can't talk very well. I've been trying to teach her."

Mr. George smiled. "That's good of you, Jesse. However, I ought to have a chat with your parents. Where do you live?"

"Over there." Jesse waved vaguely towards the channel.

"So, you came across the channel. You know there's a school on your island?"

Jesse nodded. "I know, but we live on the north end and it's hard getting around because the roads are so bad."

"But it won't be difficult for me to go over and meet your parents one day?"

"Yes, it will," Jesse practically shouted. "My mom lives in Vancouver now and my dad works all day with a logging crew."

"How did you come this morning?" Mr. George asked gently.

"We came by ourselves.... I mean, Dad dropped us off and... and he was in a big rush." Jesse felt the blood pouring into his face.

"Don't worry, Jesse. We can talk about it later. Why don't you join the others at the table — we're doing a project on marine mammals."

Jesse watched from the corner of his eye as Mr. George went to sit down beside Merle. If only she stayed peaceful.

"Hi," a girl's voice said. "I'm Sal, Woody's sister. Want to see this book about whales?"

Jesse felt his face changing shade. He was a ripe tomato, a red balloon about to burst over the table.... "We've got a whale in our cove," he finally blurted out.

"You have?" Sal and the others pounced on him. "How big is he? Have you seen him eating? Can we go there? Hope he doesn't swim away."

Jesse heard himself talking — he was actually talking to a whole bunch of kids, while Mr. George hovered nearby, listening.

When lunch hour rolled around, Jesse and Merle and the twins hurried down to the store and bought the biggest container of ice cream they could find.

"This is living," Woody sighed, scooping out mouthful after mouthful, then letting the crunchy bits dissolve on his tongue. He stopped once to burp.

"You're revolting," Sal complained.

"Can't help it. Too full. Half a peanut butter sandwich anyone?"

"Sure, hand it over." Jesse sprawled on the dock, munching peanut butter and listening to the water sucking at the tubeworms and seaweed fronds attached to the pilings.

In the middle of a slurp Merle jumped up and flapped both arms towards the channel. The ice cream dripped down her chin onto her T-shirt and jeans.

"Click, click..." Raza stopped at the buoy marking the entrance to Shelter Bay. "Large bay ahead, dock, lots of fish boats. They turned in here, I think."

Flora craned her neck. "If I'm not mistaken I see them now, sitting on the dock."

"What'll we do? Too many humans. Too many comings and goings."

"I hadn't expected such heavy traffic," Flora admitted, watching another boat chug past. "I think you ought to lie low while I venture closer to spy on the youngsters."

"Whoosh...too boring. I'm always staying, you're always going."

"It won't be so boring if you keep spouting waterfalls like that last one."

"Sorry, it comes naturally. But I'll lie low if you want." Raza watched as the grey goose paddled towards shore.

Sal shaded her eyes against the sun's glare. "It looks like a whale blowing. How did you know it was there, Merle? I never heard or saw a thing."

Merle flapped her hands. "Whale...whale."

"It must be that whale I was telling you about remember?" Jesse frowned. All he needed now was a whale following him around. Norm would hear for sure.

"No kidding!" Woody said. "First a whale appears in your front yard, then it starts tagging after you like an overgrown pooch. There's a mystery here, Jesse. Captain Crunch may be way off the mark on landings, but if there's a mystery to solve..."

"Oh sure, and don't forget the goose, who follows the whale, who follows the boat! Forget it, Woody."

"A goose — is that the one you mean?" Sal pointed towards a grey goose heading their way.

Jesse gulped. What was going on? "Yeah, that's the same bird who floated into our cove."

"Well, she looks exactly like the goose I lost," Sal continued, "and if she swims closer I'll know for positive. I've been looking everywhere."

Woody clapped his hands. "Fantastic! The plot thickens with feathers. What do you think, Merle? You hear everything."

Merle raced around the dock, waving and swooping her arms. Suddenly she crumpled to the ground with a high-pitched squeal.

"What's wrong with her?" Woody asked.

"Don't ask me." Jesse leaned over his sister and whispered, "Merle, stand up. And don't act silly."

"Silly... silly, Jesse." Merle bit her lip until it was bleeding, then wiped the blood on her T-shirt.

"Quit it, Merle, you're hurting yourself. How can you go back to school like that?"

Sal pulled a kleenex from her jean's pocket and held it against Merle's lip. "She's trying to tell us something, aren't you, Merle? Is somebody hurt?"

Merle smiled at Sal and made a loud noise with her tongue. Clack! The noise echoed around the pilings, scaring the tube worms into their shells.

"That's a super sound," Sal told her. "Can you do it again, Merle?"

Merle leaned over the water and clacked her tongue three more times. A school of sea perch lounging under the dock dove for safer waters.

"Hey, look at the whale out there," Woody yelled, racing to the end of the dock. "He's poking his head above the water and staring right at us. Wait till we tell Mr. George."

"Are we ever dumb!" Sal said, turning to Jesse. "But thanks to Merle we've finally got it."

"What do you mean got it. Got what? I haven't got a thing."

"Merle means your whale is hurt, at least I think that's what she is trying to say."

"And now he's holing up in your cove trying to get better," Woody finished triumphantly.

"I dunno..." Jesse hesitated. "And don't call him my whale. He's not my whale."

"Wounded and sick animals do the weirdest things," Sal continued, "like hiding or creeping off by themselves."

"To die," Jesse added gloomily.

Woody shook his watch and thumped it against the dock. "Quit again. And I bet we're late for school. Come on you three."

Raza dozed beyond the buoy, listening to the sea sounds — waves stroking the rocks, barnacles breathing, fish sifting through the kelp beds. And from further away came the rollicking shore sounds.

"Whumph, too long. What's keeping that goose?" Raza watched a line of fish boats turn into the bay. "Click, click... hear her coming now. And about time," he whistled.

"The time does seem interminable," Flora agreed. "I've been watching them eating something messy on the dock. You wouldn't believe the spilling, slopping, splashing."

"I heard them licking and slurping. Too bad old bull isn't here to whack them one."

"To change the subject," Flora asked, "have you ever watched a goose's marvellous eating mechanism?"

Raza yawned. "Too much bother. Can't get close enough to see."

"You won't see a false move," Flora persisted. "Sight the field, side swipe the blade of grass, snip and swallow — simple as that. No garbage, no unsightly stumps, no blood or gore."

Raza sprung his huge jaws open. "Go on, take a good look. Step inside. Ever seen such teeth?"

"Admirable for slashing and tearing, I expect." Flora's honk echoed around the cavernous mouth. "Phew, let me out!"

Raza rolled her out on his tongue. "Scared, eh?"

The grey goose ruffled her feathers into place. "Scared? Certainly not. I was momentarily overcome by your inside dimensions and the smell of fish. Certainly not scared."

"I bet you don't like my looks. You think I'm ugly."

Raza slowly sunk his head. "You never saw me in my good days — back flipping, lobtailing, spin diving. Now I'm a run-down, broken-fluked..."

"Whoa back!" Flora honked. "I can see everything in my mind's eye and you look simply splendid in your shining black and whiteness."

"Wheee... I do?"

"You most certainly, certainly do. And one of these days when you are feeling like your old self I shall watch you with my ordinary eye," she promised.

"You will?" The joy of the promise spun Raza into a back flip. "Squee... it hurts everytime I move. What if I can't follow them anymore?"

"Sh, simmer down. I spy a whole flock of human youngsters racing towards the dock."

"I hear them too. Flipping and flopping like a school of fish."

"Don't forget to check your whale for injuries," Woody shouted from the dock. "And we'll be waiting for you tomorrow — same time, same place. Don't be late."

After helping Merle into the boat, Jesse untied the ropes and pushed off. There was no time to waste. Norm would be leaving work soon and if he arrived back to find the boat gone and nobody home, he'd have a fit.

"See you, Woody." Jesse yanked the starting cord and shifted the engine into reverse. At least I hope so. Too many things could go wrong before tomorrow rolled around.

Once they had cleared the end of the dock and the boats moored there, Jesse shifted into full speed. Merle covered her ears as the boat lunged forward.

"Fast, Jesse... fast."

Jesse didn't pay any attention. If Woody and Sal are right

about the whale being hurt, he kept thinking, why doesn't it stay put? Why does it keep following us?

"Bad, bad, Jesse." Merle was beside him, tugging at the arm holding the engine.

"What's wrong now?" Jesse cut the engine.

Merle didn't say a word, only smiled, when the boat slowed down.

"Merle, I can't wait all afternoon. If you won't tell me what's wrong I'm starting the engine again. We're in a hurry, remember?"

"Uh, huh, Jesse. Uh, huh."

"Instead of bothering me, Merle, why don't you keep a lookout for whales or driftwood or anything else that might get in our way."

Funny little kid. In two seconds she could change from sad into happy. Would she always stay the same Merle or would she grow up like everything else? Never mind. I'll always look after you, Merle. And I guess that means looking after your whale and your goose, too.

As the shadow of the opposite shore overtook them, Jesse shivered and ducked inside his hood. He cut the engine and let the boat slide against their dock. Good, there was no sign of Norm yet.

"Merle, stay with the boat. Don't move. I'll run up to the cabin and get some antibiotic stuff we can rub on the whale in case we find anything infected."

Merle nodded her head. She closed her eyes and listened to Raza and Flora turning into the cove.

"Make sure you don't move," Jesse called back.

Raza spyhopped. "Running, always running. Where's the boy going now?"

"Swim closer, the situation warrants investigation. And

84

I must say you're a fine one to complain about someone else running around!"

"He makes me tired. Very, very tired."

Near shore Raza listened to the littleneck clams siphoning water through their shells — in and out, in and out. Merle breathed with them. Raza watched as she stretched out her hand to stroke the grey goose's feathers.

"I've got it," Jesse yelled, almost slipping off the cedar logs. "Hold the tube, Merle, but don't squeeze too hard — the stuff is oozing out."

In the excitement Jesse dropped the oars. "Do you think we've scared the whale away?"

Merle laughed and shook her head. When they were in deeper water she leaned over and blew onto the surface.

"Careful," Jesse warned.

As Merle's face touched the water, ripples formed and spread into a circle. A huge head rose in the centre and there was the whale staring at them. Jesse stretched his hand out, then jerked back. Where the bullets had grazed the whale's skin, a slimy, grey ooze had formed.

Jesse shuddered. "His back looks all infected. What if he won't stay still while we're rubbing the antibiotic ointment on? You try first, Merle. I think he trusts you."

Merle smeared the gooeyness over her hands, sniffed it and made a face when some landed on her nose. Then very gently she smoothed the ointment over the whale's back.

Flora peered into one of Raza's eyes. "Does it sting? Can you hold still?"

"Her hands are soft and cool. But the white stuff burns with the sharpness of a broken barnacle shell. I'd like to leap and spin and roar."

Flora patted him with one wing. "Now, now... we sea creatures must be brave."

A wisp of something grey flowed from the whale's eye. "Squee, so the old ones always said. But now I hurt and I'm all alone."

"What?" Flora honked. "You mean to say I'm nothing, the girl is nothing, the boy..."

"Stop...sorry. The trouble is I'm not getting better. Scared and lonely feeling."

"Whatever they are doing will surely help. Humans perform the most amazing feats nowadays. And listen, Merle is singing especially for you."

"I like her sound," Raza squeaked. "It reminds me of something a long, long time ago. She's beautiful for a human, isn't she?"

"Hmmph...probably, probably. They say beauty is only skin deep, but I fancy her beauty goes deeper."

While Jesse held the boat steady, Merle rubbed more ointment over the whale's back and sang:

> *Iceburn, fireburn,*
> *Twist and turn.*
> *Circle round*
> *Spin and sound,*
> *Back on home*
> *And hold your own.*

Why doesn't she hurry, Jesse grumbled to himself. "Come on, Merle. Save some of the antibiotic stuff for tomorrow. Dad will be home any minute."

With a few strokes of the oars Jesse swung their boat against the dock. Merle crawled along the cedar logs on her hands and knees, then sat down and wouldn't budge.

"Let's go, Merle. The whale will be okay — I promise."

"No."

As Jesse bent down to lift her, the grey goose waddled

up, flapping its wings. Merle flapped too, until her jacket sleeves whistled in the wind.

Jesse stroked Flora's head. "You're a good, sensible goose. I like geese. Are you coming? I bet you'd like a nice crust of bread when we get home."

The three of them walked and waddled to the cabin while Raza watched from the cove, pressed as close to shore as he dared, wishing for a pair of legs — any kind of legs — so that he might walk with them, too.

Bad Day

When Jesse stepped inside the cabin and slipped off his jacket, he could feel the chill. It was five o'clock and the sun had left their clearing several hours ago. Norm would be home anytime. Jesse quickly stuffed some paper and kindling into the stove, lit it and put the same old pot of clam chowder on to warm.

"Take a sniff and see what you think, Merle."

By mistake she dunked her whole nose in the pot. "Poof," she giggled, wrinkling her nose and wiping it on one sleeve. "Poof."

"Quit making those noises, Merle. I don't like the smell either, but it will do for tonight's dinner, as long as we can think of something better for tomorrow."

89

Afterwards Jesse took the smaller of the two chainsaws from the woodshed and started working on the downed maple tree. One by one, Merle carted the huge chunks that he was cutting and dropped them outside the shed. Then Norm would use their heaviest maul to split the wood into small pieces before stacking it away.

Norm arrived home in the middle of the chainsawing. "How's everything?" he asked, flopping down on the maple stump.

"We haven't got very far with this tree," Jesse apologized, "too busy with other things I guess." Not exactly the truth, but not a hundred percent lie either. Now as long as Merle didn't drop a hint of where they'd been all day....

The three were too tired to talk over supper. Merle stirred and stirred her chowder, spilling more with each stir, until finally she fell asleep over the table.

"This chowder has seen better days," Norm remarked, quitting halfway through his bowl.

"Tomorrow I'll jig for rock cod," Jesse promised, "and catch us some supper, with luck."

"Whale-luck," Merle mumbled half asleep.

Jesse gave her a little kick under the table.

"Don't forget our pizza dinner next Saturday night," Norm reminded them.

"How could we forget, Dad?"

Norm pushed his chair back. "If you don't mind, Jesse, I think I'll turn in early tonight. Our boss is really high-balling the logging operation. I know he wants to be done before winter hits the hills, but the constant pressure makes a fellow weary."

As he left the table he patted Merle on the head. "How's it going all day by yourselves?"

"Fine, Dad. Just great." Jesse felt another pinch of guilt for what he didn't say.

"Well, Jesse... I've been thinking. All day with the chainsaw buzzing and shaking and with the timber crashing down, I've been trying to think. And it seems to me that you two might be better off with your mother for a while. I'd send money each month, enough so Merle could go to one of those special schools your mother was talking about. It might get lonely here, but..."

"Listen, Dad," Jesse interrupted, "we want to stay here. Don't we Merle? I haven't lived in the city since I was a tiny kid. We'd miss everything — we'd miss you, Dad. How would you make dinner all alone?"

Norm caught them up in his arms and danced around the cabin until they dropped down dizzy on Merle's bunk bed.

"We'll talk about plans over the weekend when I have more time. How's that, Jesse?"

Later, curled up inside his sleeping bag, Jesse listened to the silence stealing around the cabin. Merle and Norm slept, the stove died down, the stream shrank in the chill night air and the fir needles hung listless. Except for the close thump, thump, thump of his heart, it was still...

Although the first, faint stirrings in the northwest were too far away to hear, the wind and the waves and the rain were gradually building into a storm. It broke against the outer coast of Vancouver Island and shook a lonely lighthouse.

Merle whimpered in her sleep. Was she having a bad dream or what? Jesse started counting heartbeats, one-two, one-two, anything to drown out his worries. If he went to school in the morning he would be digging himself deeper and deeper into trouble. Mr. George would visit them, Norm would hear he had taken the boat and what a mess! On the other hand if he dropped the whole school business right now, everything would go back to normal. "But I want to go tomorrow. I promised Woody. He'll be waiting for me."

Perhaps he should tell Norm about school, say he was sorry for taking the boat and promise not to break the rules again. There was a water taxi, wasn't there? It could detour to pick them up...

But Jesse could hear Norm's anger rising like a tidal wave roaring up a narrow inlet. "You sneaked off in the boat? You know southeasters blow straight up the main channel. You know, one little mistake out there is enough. Why do you think I made that bloody rule about not going alone into the main channel — for fun?"

"I know, Dad, but there wasn't a ripple on the water."

Arguing only made Norm madder. "Enough! I don't want to hear another word."

I can't risk telling him, Jesse decided. I can't lose tomorrow. Woody is counting on me. I promised I'd be there. Later, sometime later, I'll tell Norm.... And Jesse fell asleep in the middle of his own conversation.

Next morning Jesse was awake before either of the alarms went off. When he crawled from his sleeping bag and smudged a pajama sleeve across the window, he saw it was as dark outside as in. Jesse tiptoed around the cabin, doing the usual morning chores, trying to feel his usual morning self. After a while he shook Merle awake.

"Not a peep about school," he warned. "Remember to be sh."

"Sssssh," Merle hissed back.

Norm switched on their battery-operated radio. "Storm force winds over the outer coast will gradually work their way into our area by this afternoon... easing to gale force over the inner coast. Small craft warnings have been issued for all waters..."

Jesse tried to shut out the announcer's voice. Why did

Norm always have to flick on that radio? Since Mom left it had become a regular habit — night and day.

"Sounds like a bad day to be out on the water," Norm remarked. "Not so great in the woods either, with all those tree tops swaying and dancing in the breeze. Don't be surprised if you see me home early, Jesse."

"Weather reports on the coast are always wrong," Jesse grumbled.

"Don't let the weather get you down," Norm said, patting him on the back. "Some people can feel pretty isolated when it rains and blows for days on end. Not me, I like it. But I should have realized how much your mother hated the winters here."

"Anything I can do around the place?" Jesse asked, trying to change the subject. He glanced at his watch. It was time — why didn't Norm leave?

"There's that maple tree to buck up and the trail to the well needs brushing out.... But if the weather turns sour, leave the outside work and we can do it together over the weekend." Norm stood up and shouldered his pack. "I better be going. See you this evening and take care."

"Bye, Dad." Finally... now there was only Merle left to worry about.

She was sitting cross-legged on the bunk bed rattling her shell necklace, the one he'd made from the most beautiful shells he could find — abalone, limpet, turban, scallop — and they tinkled together like wind-swung bells.

"Merle, how come you aren't up? I thought you'd be all dressed. Would you like some orange juice? Merle, I asked you something and you aren't listening. I said ORANGE JUICE!"

Merle shook her head. "Uh, huh. Uh, huh." The roaring of the distant storm broke inside her head, blocking out Jesse's voice. In her hands the shells rattled like skeletons.

"It's no use," Jesse muttered, "she can't hear me." When he opened the cabin door to peek at the weather he could hardly tell where sky and sea met, it was so still and grey and changed from the day before. The whale and the goose were hidden somewhere in that greyness.

At least there was no wind, yet. Jesse closed the door and hurried back to Merle. "If we want to meet Woody and Sal we better go. Don't you want to see them, Merle? And what about the whale and the goose?"

Merle's head shook like the top of a fir tree in a storm.

Jesse waited for ages.... We shouldn't go. We should. Didn't you hear the weather report? Don't believe it — weather reports are mostly wrong. Then let's go before the wind builds up. But I can't get her to listen. She won't move. "PLEASE MERLE."

Gradually she uncurled herself from the bunk bed and stretched her arms and legs.

"Come on, Merle, take your hand off your ears so I can pull this sweater on.... Now sit still and I'll bring some porridge. I made it how you like it, smooth as jelly. Just a few mouthfuls to warm your insides, okay?"

"Uh, huh, Jesse. Uh, huh." Merle stuck her fingers in both ears again.

"What's wrong, Merle, aren't you hungry? If you feel sick or anything tell me and we'll stay home."

"Uh, huh. Uh, huh." Merle kept sucking air in and out of her mouth like a stranded fish. Tiny bubbles grew on her lips, then popped before they were big enough to fly away.

Jesse talked to fill the grey and empty space inside the cabin. He talked while he made peanut butter and jam sandwiches and filled his pack, he talked while he zipped Merle's jacket and struggled with her boots, until the cabin door closed behind them he went on talking...

"Squee, whee... where are they heading?" Raza wiggled both flippers. "Don't ask me to follow. I'm not going anywhere. Too early."

"The early bird catches the worm," Flora observed. "And seeing the youngsters are carrying packs and a fishing rod, I suspect it means another boat trip."

"Too bad," Raza whistled. "Too bad. I feel something big coming our way."

"You do? What precisely do you feel? Come on — enlarge, elaborate, spell it out for me."

"A roaring in my head, a far off shaking of the waters. Something different — you know."

"I don't know. How can a creature of sight and surfaces know what you know? Tell me the how and why of it."

"Too long, too hard, too boring. The old ones knew about weather, days and days ahead..."

"Unfortunately they aren't here to tell me," Flora snapped. "Now about this storm or whatever it is you are predicting."

"Aw, what's a little storm? Stay below and listen to the roar."

"There are some among us who are neither water, nor underwater creatures," Flora reminded him, waving one wing towards the dock.

Raza spyhopped and saw Merle sitting in the boat and Jesse strugging with the starting cord. "Squee... stop the minnow-heads. They're sailing smack into the storm."

"Probably too late," the grey goose honked, struggling to get herself airborne. "Afraid so, afraid so."

Raza flung himself in front of the boat, but it swerved away.

"Dumb whale," Jesse yelled back. "You almost caused an accident."

"Bad, bad, Jesse." But Merle's cry was swallowed up in the engine's roar.

"You heard him?" Raza squealed. "He'll crash, he'll smash, he'll bash..."

"He is overwrought," Flora concluded.

"Whumph... he'll soon be overboard."

"Overwrought, overboard, or whatever, I say we ought to follow their boat."

"Squee... so, so sleepy. Feel terrible. What's wrong with me?"

The grey goose circumnavigated the whale and stopped beside his head. "What I see I don't like. There is a grey ooze seeping from your wounds and enveloping the healthy skin." She checked both eyes. "Like I thought, lacking their usual life and lustre. How's your appetite?"

Raza opened and shut his mouth a few times. "Put a fish inside and I'd swallow, I guess."

"But no outburst of enthusiasm?"

Raza shook his head. "Too tired."

"Now listen carefully; beside the stream that empties into the cove there are healing herbs growing. Tonight I shall snip a few and chew them into a salve to spread over your wounds."

"Sounds terrible..." Raza started to squeak. "I mean thank you Flora. You're nice — very, very nice."

"You sound all wrong," the grey goose chattered. "Terribly, terribly wrong. What's required if you ask me, is rest and recuperation."

Raza shook his huge head. "Not that sick. Not yet. The grey goose won't swim alone."

And side by side, the whale and the goose swam after the boat.

Southeaster

"Made it," Jesse shouted, standing up in the boat as they swerved into Shelter Bay. "And you know what, Merle? I don't think it's going to storm. That weather forecaster from Vancouver is never right."

Merle waved her arms in spins and dives and figure-eights.

"Quit imitating that stupid whale, Merle. You saw how he plunked himself down in front of our boat. It was lucky we didn't hit him."

Merle banged her fists against the side of the boat until her knuckles were red. Jesse pretended not to notice.

"We're too early," he said, cutting the engine. "It'll be another half hour before the water taxi arrives. Let's drift around in the bay and jig for cod and maybe we'll catch some supper."

After tying a weight on the line, Jesse baited the hook with a piece of clam and let it sink to the bottom. "Hold the rod, Merle, while I stow Dad's fishing box away. And keep moving the line up and down like there's something alive on the end."

"Ow...Jesse, ow." The rod was bent double and Merle was almost overboard.

Jesse grabbed the line. "You've hooked onto something huge, Merle. It feels like a halibut." Someday he was heading north to fish for halibut — the giant kind you had to winch into the boat. A flash of red broke the surface.

"Snapper," Jesse yelled. "You've caught a beauty, Merle. Where's the net? Help me flip him in. Watch he doesn't catch on the edge. Careful."

Merle smiled. The sound of the flapping fish drowned out the other sounds.

"What a beaut!" Jesse kept saying. "There's enough fish here for two or three dinners. Will Norm ever be pleased." He took in the loose line, attached the hook so it wouldn't snag anything and stowed the rod away. "I guess we can quit the fishing."

When he stood up a moment later he saw Merle lifting the fish in both arms and holding it over the whale's gaping mouth. "Merle... don't!"

With one gulp the fish was gone. Merle smiled and patted the ugly beast's snout before it ducked under water.

"Merle, how could you?"

With one violent wrench of the starting cord he got the engine going. Woody and Sal and the other kids waved from the water taxi as it sped past, but Jesse kept both hands clenched on the tiller. He didn't cut the engine soon enough and the boat crunched against the dock.

"You better eat your breakfast sandwich now, Merle. It's all you're getting till lunch."

While he was fiddling with the ropes Merle crumbled the sandwich and smeared it over her jeans. Gradually the smell of peanut butter hit Jesse.

"MERLE!"

He grabbed an oily rag and tried to wipe off the peanut butter and jam, but the mixture only soaked deeper into her jeans. Finally Jesse flopped onto the dock. What was the point of going to school or doing anything today? Woody and Sal waved, but he couldn't be bothered moving.

"Anything wrong?" Woody shouted down. "We didn't think you'd come today. You heard the small craft warning?"

"I don't listen to weather forecasters anymore," Jesse mumbled. "They wear umbrellas instead of hats."

Woody sniffed. "Something reeks."

"Yeah...her. Peanut butter and jam and engine oil smeared over jeans."

"Whew, what a recipe!"

"Well, there's more. Before you came she fed a huge red snapper we'd just caught to that whale. And look at her now, crumbling sandwich all over the boat. Quit it, Merle."

"What's bugging her?"

"Don't ask me," Jesse snapped. "Aren't you the great detective?"

"Did you find anything wrong with the whale?" Woody asked, changing the subject.

"Sure, his back is covered with cuts and the pain is probably driving him crazy. You know what happened this morning? As we were leaving he swam right in front of the boat. We almost collided."

Jesse waited for one of Woody's Captain Crunch jokes, but his friend kept quiet.

"I think the whale was trying to tell you something," Sal chimed in.

"What do you mean?"

"Maybe the whale was worried and he..."

"Oh great," Jesse interrupted. "Willy, the Worried Whale — some story."

"Boy, are you ever crabby," Woody complained. "I'm leaving. Coming Sal?"

As they walked away, Merle thumped the side of the boat. "Whumph!" The whale surfaced nearby and the grey goose honked.

"Sal is right," Woody shouted back. "And it looks like you've got a worried goose too."

"Wait a second." Jesse ran after Woody and grabbed his arm. "What exactly do you mean by worried?"

"Ever seen a dog that sniffs and knows everything, trying to tell his clueless owner a thing or two?"

"I dunno... maybe."

"Well, whales have even huger brains than dogs and seeing as they are pack animals too, they'll try and look after..."

"You don't mean ME?"

"Could be," Woody replied, without waiting around to finish the conversation.

Jesse couldn't concentrate on his school work that day. Too many other thoughts were churning inside his head. Worries about Norm, his mom, Merle, the whale and now Woody and Sal kept surfacing. Were his new friends mad at him?

There was also the weather. A southeaster was starting to shake the trees and slap cedar boughs against the roof. It rode the whitecaps, line after line of them down the channel. Jesse grew dizzy watching through the window.

Mr. George wandered over. "I had a look at the correspondence papers you brought me, Jesse. Excellent work. You're ahead in everything except math. But I'd still like to have a chat with your father. How's this weekend?"

Jesse felt his throat squeezing shut. "We're going into town." And it wasn't a lie either.

"Well, if I happen to be heading down your way I may stop on the chance you're home."

DON'T! Jesse came close to screaming. The sound struggled inside his throat, like the southeaster outside the building.

Merle sat by the window whirling her hands round and round the pane in a whining sound. Once she touched the glass with her tongue, but that was soft and silent. Rain began to slide down the window.

Sometime in the early afternoon a door banged below and footsteps clumped up the stairs. "Sorry for interrupting you, Mr. George, but I'd like to get the students home early today. The wind is building up and it's no weather for small boats."

"Homework, raingear, life jackets...." Mr. George reminded everyone. "Have a good weekend and see you on Monday if the wind has calmed down. Now wait a minute...Penny, Jackson, Daniel and the rest of you Shelter Bay-ites, there's no sneaking off early for you kids."

Outside, the rain, blown sideways by the southeaster, pinged against their raingear and stung their faces. Jesse took Merle by one arm and half swung her along the road.

"It's wild out there," Woody shouted when they reached the dock. "And you'll be heading straight into the southeaster. Don't be crazy, Jesse. Leave your boat tied here and come with us in the water taxi."

"Look Woody, I have to get this boat home. I never told you...my dad doesn't know we are here. He'll murder me if he ever finds out where I've taken our boat."

"Maybe he won't notice the boat is missing."

"No chance—he's got the whole weekend to notice."

"Sounds like your dad is some kind of people-eater."

"He is not. You don't know him, Woody. He gets mad when people break the rules — that's all."

"Sorry, just kidding. I have to go, the guy from the water taxi is waving. Take care, eh?"

And then Merle and he were alone on the dock, waving to the water taxi until it disappeared beyond the point.

"I'll zip up your life jacket, Merle."

Two-thirty. No time to waste. And with such foul weather there was a good chance Norm would be leaving work early. Jesse checked the fuel tank. Still a third full, that should see them home safely. Reconnect fuel line to engine, pump up pressure, pull out choke—reciting the list helped calm him down. Oars stowed properly, rope and extra floater ring handy...

"Merle, it will be too rough up front. Take the extra tarp and life jacket and go sit on the floor. I know it's not so comfy there, but I can't help it. We're in a big hurry now."

The engine started on the first pull. Soon Shelter Bay, the docks, the fish boats, were disappearing behind them in the wind and rain. The closer they came to the buoy and open water, the faster Jesse's heart pounded, and as if keeping time, Merle's feet tapped against the bottom of the boat.

"Click...click." Raza heard the tapping and surfaced in the lee of the headland where the grey goose was floating. He held a fish crossways in his mouth. "I found it floating on the surface, half dead. Want a bite?"

Flora shook her head. "Your need is greater than mine."

Raza bit the fish in two and spat out the head half. Must be the snapper he'd swallowed earlier. Not hungry at all. "Click, click...message from the girl. They're heading home now. Minnow-brains! Listen to the waves."

Flora shivered. "A few minutes ago I watched a whole boatload of youngsters heading into the storm. Why don't humans follow the example of us creatures and stay put in such foul weather?"

"Don't ask me," Raza squeaked. "Storm...stay below. That's what old bull always said."

"And not all of us are so versatile underwater," Flora reminded him again.

"Seaweed-brain!" Raza groaned, whacking his head on the water. "I keep forgetting. What's wrong with me?"

"Your brain is functioning admirably. The old ones would be proud of you and so am I."

"Squee, whee...through storm and high water I shall lead us. How's that sound?"

"Remarkable, except for one little problem. How do I stay with you through storm and high water?"

"Easy as swallowing a snapper. Climb on my back. Grab my dorsal fin with your grass-gnashers. Ouch, not so hard. Watch out, here they come. And hold tight. Here we gooo..."

Jesse slowed the engine when they reached the buoy marking the entrance to Shelter Bay. "Hold tight, Merle, here we go."

The first big wave caught the bow and sent spray sailing over them. As the boat lurched forward, another wave reflecting off the headland caught and held them in a deep trough. Water poured over the sides.

"Jesse..." Merle bawled from her tarp.

"Stay where you are. Don't move, Merle."

As the next wave lifted them and seemed about to smash them against the rocks, Jesse gave the engine a touch more gas. "Go, little boat. Don't stall now." It was working. The extra momentum surfed their boat along the wave's crest, finally landing them in calmer waters beyond the headland.

Jesse started laughing. "I can't help it, Merle. Your head looks so funny sticking out from that tarp."

The more he laughed, the louder Merle howled. "Oow, Jesse...all wet."

"Squee...what's going on here?" Raza spluttered, rounding the headland and entering calmer water.

"Full speed ahead to investigate," Flora tried to say, but she couldn't open her beak while holding on.

"Can't talk, eh?" Raza clapped one flipper. "Ouch, stop chewing my dorsal fin. I'm going, I'm going..."

Still weak from laughing, Jesse fumbled around for a bailing can. He found one, squeezed and half crushed, between the fuel tanks.

Merle stretched out her hands. "Pul-eese, Jesse."

Why not? Anything to keep her quiet. "But you have to bail really fast, Merle. Watch how I do it."

A can of water hit the whale smack in the snout. "Whumph," Raza snorted.

Merle giggled and Jesse jumped back like he had been stung by a wasp. The whale was grinning. And so was the grey goose balancing on his back. Darn it, they were all laughing at him!

"Go ahead, bail," Jesse grumbled. "I'm supposed to run the boat, check the charts, watch for waves, look after whales and everybody else." He glanced at his watch. Three-thirty and they hadn't even crossed the channel!

Jesse lost all track of time as they dodged from one headland to the next. A couple of the floor rivets had popped out and now whenever they hit a big wave the bottom of the boat heaved up and down. "Hold together just for today," he prayed. "And I promise to fix you when we get home."

Jesse nosed the boat behind a rocky islet that he recognized from earlier trips with Norm. Although he couldn't see anything through the wind and rain, their cove lay more or less directly across the channel. Jesse checked the fuel tank and engine connection one last time. Everything seemed shipshape.

"Okay, Merle, this is it. We're crossing over."

Even though Jesse was braced for the shock, the first huge wave spun them sideways. He wrestled with the tiller and angled the bow into the wind again. What if another boat was coming up the channel and he didn't see it? No idiot would be out in this weather...oh yeah, what was he doing? The salt spray stung his eyes and seeped down the back of his neck. He still couldn't see the opposite shore. Hold the boat steady, keep her pointing at the right angle, watch for any freak waves....His hands were shaking from the cold and the strain of gripping the tiller.

How's little Merle? As Jesse glanced down, a wave lifted the prow of their boat and flung them broadside on. They landed with a sickening thud, water sloshing over the sides. The engine spluttered, then came again with a roar. Was it driftwood or seaweed tangled in the propellor? Jesse squinted his eyes through the whiteness of wind-driven rain and spray. Something dark loomed ahead. Their own headland? But it was way too close. The motor faltered again, then conked out for good.

"Throw off the tarp, Merle. Get your legs free. Hold on...I'm coming."

A wave reflecting off the headland struck the side of their boat and rolled Jesse overboard.

"Jesse," Merle screamed. "Jesse."

No answer.

Then she called another name. "Raza...Raza."

"Click, click...boy overboard," Raza screeched. "I knew it—boy overboard. I hear the girl, but I don't see or hear the boy. Stick with the boat, Flora."

As Jesse fell, his head hit something hard. Water poured into his boots. He kicked them off and struggled towards the boat. Through the wind he could hear Merle calling "Jesse...Jesse," and then, "Raza," whatever that meant. Another wave washed over him and there was only darkness and a distant roaring.

From below, Raza could see the boy's legs swinging back and forth. He nudged them gently, half expecting a kick in return. No sound or movement came from the boy—only the lifejacket was holding him upright. Raza took the body in his mouth, but feeling the softness a-gainst the sharpness of his own teeth, he panicked. "Squee...whee, can't!"

"Raza, Raza." If it hadn't been for Merle calling and calling his name he might have dropped the thing.

"Sw-swim," the grey goose ordered. "Swim like you never have before."

And Raza swam through the whiteness of wind and rain and waves, holding in his jaws that soft thing which threatened at any moment to fall apart.

"Swim...swim for your life," came the faraway echo. Was it the old ones telling him what to do?

And he swam forever, to a point just inside the headland where the water grew calmer.

Jesse felt a sharp piercing in his left side. Was it a rock, a torn oyster shell, a barnacle? His fingers dug into rock, his muscles strained to gain a hold. Something immensely powerful was shoving him and then flipping him onto a grassy bench beyond the water's reach. That done, the whale slipped under the water again.

While Jesse lay on his stomach gasping for breath, he heard someone calling, "Merle, where are you?" Then everything else faded, except the "Merle" sounding in his ears.

Beyond the headland the water grew wild again. "Where are you? Where are you?" Raza whistled. The boat was drifting overturned, and the girl and the grey goose were gone.

Raza dove under the storm. Nothing there. Wait a minute. What was that faint sound? "Click, click...girl floating down wind. Arms wrapped around goose's neck. Still alive."

Raza surfaced with the two of them on his back. "Hold fast. We'll swim to shore."

"What a hero," Flora honked, "undoubtedly, undeniably, a hero. We're proud of you."

"Proud of you...proud of you," came the distant, underwater echo.

And Merle sang with the wind blowing her hair straight out:

> Raza be nimble
> Raza be quick...

On shore Jesse stirred and tried to roll over. Who was singing?

Footsteps crackled through the salal bushes above him. "Jesse, where are you?" Norm shouted. "JESSE...if that whale has hurt anyone I'll kill him. I'll pump a hundred bullets into his mangy hide."

Jesse pushed himself onto his elbows. "Don't hurt the whale, Dad. He brought me home."

Norm was bending over him, pressing one hand tight against his forehead to stop the flow of blood. "Poor little guy, poor little guy."

Jesse struggled to sit up. "Where's Merle?"

Norm held him back. "I think everything is under control, Jesse. The trouble is, I can't believe my own eyes. Look there."

Jesse turned his head. The whale was swimming towards shore with Merle and the grey goose balanced on his back. The goose was honking and Merle was singing with the wind blowing her hair straight out:

> Raza be nimble,
> Raza be quick...

Circle Round

The next morning Jesse woke up with a head that felt like a battered drift log. Besides having a headache, he was stiff all over. He didn't even remember going to bed. Norm must have put him there. He peered at his watch. Ten-thirty. So much for their plans of going to town. Anyhow, it didn't matter because he felt too rotten for shopping or eating pizza.

Jesse leaned over the edge of his sleeping platform. Nobody down there. But outside the sun was shining, a winter wren was bubbling its song and it was practically the middle of the day. "I hate sleeping in," he grumbled.

Suddenly there were footsteps and voices outside the cabin. Who was it? Jesse flattened himself on the foamie and pulled the sleeping bag over his head. He didn't want to see anyone; most of all he didn't want to see Norm or hear any of his questions. What was the crazy idea taking that boat out in the middle of a southeaster, eh Jesse? Come on. I want the whole story. The voice inside his head grew louder. Or was it Norm's voice outside the cabin? Jesse threw off the sleeping bag.

"It's too bad Jesse missed you," Norm was saying. "He was sound asleep when I checked him earlier. I hated to wake him."

"Better to let him sleep after the terrible day he had yesterday," Mr. George agreed.

"Mr. George!" Jesse's heart sank through his sleeping bag and smothered inside the foamie.

"And thanks for dropping by," Norm continued. "Your ideas about school and finding someone to help with Merle sound good. I'll talk it over with Jesse this weekend."

So Norm knew the whole story already and they would be talking things over...

"I'll walk down to the dock and see you off," Norm offered.

"Good and don't anyone bother coming back," Jesse mumbled into his pillow. "I'm not getting up."

Jesse had just pulled the sleeping bag back over his head when more voices arrived. What a racket! For some reason Merle kept calling the grey goose. "Goosey, goosey. Here goosey." Why didn't the whole world shut up and leave him alone?

"It's Flora all right. I can tell," Woody announced triumphantly. "Fat as ever and hitting rock bottom when she waddles. Right, Sal?"

"Why don't you run down to the beach and get lost, Woody?"

"I'm already on my way," Woody shouted. "Where's

Jesse? You see him anywhere?''

"He's not feeling well after the boat accident. Weren't you listening down on the beach when his dad told us? He said Jesse was still sleeping. And now you've probably gone and woken him up with your squeaky voice.''

"Sorr-ee, Sally. See you later.''

"Goosey...goosey...'' Merle kept repeating.

"Here Flora, Flora,'' Sal crooned. "Don't worry, I'm taking you home. And I won't let my dad touch you. Nobody's going to pluck out your feathers for some old pillow or down jacket.''

Jesse sat up. "They can't have my goose. She floated in with the tide. She belongs to Merle and me.'' Jesse looked through his window. Sal and Merle were bending over the grey goose stroking her feathers. And now Merle was taking Sal by the hand, pulling her away.

"Sal...come, Sal.''

"Don't trust her, Merle. She wants our goose. Don't you give our goose away. I better get down there before everything goes wrong,'' Jesse figured. "And I should find the whale.''

He'd forgotten all about the whale. That's what happened when you got so crabby. And it was the whale who had saved him!

Jesse slipped on his jeans and T-shirt and climbed down the ladder, being careful not to joggle his aching head. Nobody around, which was just as well. He didn't want to meet Norm—not yet. After downing a glass of orange juice, Jesse grabbed a piece of bread and jam and went outside. Norm was down on the beach talking to some strange man—Woody and Sal's dad probably.

Woody was jumping up and down on the dock, trying to make it rock. "Neat floating dock,'' he yelled.

111

"Hope he falls off before he finds my raft," Jesse muttered. That guy was a menace.

Far out in the cove Jesse could see the whale swimming back and forth, back and forth, between the headlands. Now the grey goose was hurrying out to meet him. What was going on? Was anything wrong?

"Say, whose neat raft is this? Can I give it a try? Is there time, Dad? Wish Jesse was around. It would be way more fun."

Time to disappear, Jesse decided. Besides, he wanted to see what was happening out in the cove. Jesse slipped behind the cabin, hoping nobody had seen him, and took the trail leading to the headland. Through dense alder and fir forest, around the skunk cabbage swamp, over bare rock knolls he ran, until the dense salal of the headland slowed him down. Where the bush thinned and the rock sloped to the sea, Jesse stopped. He could see two people sitting below him — Merle and Sal. Why had Merle brought her to their favourite spot?

"I'll go back," Jesse thought. "They haven't seen me yet."

But Sal turned and stared at him as though she had heard his thoughts. She pointed to the water below where the whale and the grey goose were swimming.

Jesse blushed and sat down.

"Hi Jesse," she said.

"Uh...hi Sal."

Interwoven with the sea sounds came the honking of the grey goose and the swoosh of the whale as he swam back and forth, back and forth...

"Trying out my strokes," Raza stopped to say. "Need more space."

112

"So whatever Merle rubbed on your back has helped. You're feeling some better?"

"A little, I guess. A little. Hard to tell in here. I need the push and pull of the open ocean, the never-ending dive, the fathomless depths...you listening?"

"Obviously I'm listening, obviously. Do I ever not listen to my friend?"

"Squee...sorry."

"It's clear to me that you are growing restless in this cove. The question is, what next?"

"What's next?" Raza echoed. "Don't know. Can't say." He resumed his swimming, back and forth, back and forth.

"Slow down," Flora honked on one of his figure eight curves. "You're making me dizzy. Pause and reflect."

"I think as I swim and I swim as I think." Raza stopped beside Flora. "Listen, do you hear anything?"

"Hear what? I hear the swooping of sea birds, the swirling of water around rocks...nothing else of matter. Nothing at all."

"Positive?"

"Positive."

"I thought I heard the old ones calling. Swim for your life, they said. Swim over the ocean and far away. Swim like you never have before. There, it comes again. Can't you hear? If only you could hear. Then I'd know for sure what to do."

"I'm trying to the best of my ability, believe me, believe me. But I was never one for underwater sounds, if you remember."

"Squee...whee, I hear the girl calling." Raza spyhopped. "Yes, she's waving to me. I knew it, I knew it! She hears them too. Now my course is clear."

"Are you sure you're interpreting the message from

the old ones correctly?" Flora asked in a trembling voice.

"Positive."

"The open ocean holds innumerable dangers for a young and untried orca."

"Untried?" Raza squeaked, smacking his tail flukes on the surface. "I rescued the boy, remember?"

"True. Magnificently and marvellously so."

"Anything wrong?" Raza peered into the grey goose's eye. "You sound a bit strange."

"I do? Yes, probably, probably I do. The fact is, I'm wondering and worrying how alone you will feel on the open ocean."

"You aren't coming? But think of the fun we'd have together."

Flora shook her head. "I would only hold you back, probably endangering your life. I'm a shore bird and I belong here. Besides, who would keep a weather eye on the two youngsters?"

"She belongs here," Sal echoed, wiping a speck from the corner of her eye.

Jesse mumbled something and stared at the waves washing the rocks.

"Sal!" Woody yelled from somewhere or other. "It's time to go. I haven't a clue where you're hiding out, but you better come. Dad's waiting in the boat and he's getting jumpier than a grasshopper and madder by the minute."

"I better go," Sal sighed. "Look after Flora. She's a good goose. And I'm glad she's staying."

"Thanks," Jesse stuttered. "Can you come again?"

"Maybe...and I'll see you at school."

"I hope so, as long as Dad lets me go."

Sal turned around and hop-skipped up the trail.

114

Merle stretched out her hand. "Pul-eese, Sal." Too late. Sal had disappeared into the bush.

Jesse sat motionless, watching the whale and the goose. After a while Merle nudged him.

"I know, Merle. I ought to get up and do something useful, but I'm scared to go back to the cabin. Now that everyone's gone Dad will have time to get furious. And I don't blame him one bit. I wrecked our boat, Merle, and the engine too. What a mess!" Jesse rested his head on his knees.

Suddenly Merle yanked a hair from his head.

"Ouch. You quit that, Merle."

"Ow, Jesse. Ow." There were tears streaking her face. She pointed to the water below.

Raza was circling around the grey goose. "Will I find my old pod? Is there a chance? Tell me, Flora."

"Listen for the faraway echo, no matter how faint," Flora advised him. "And before you turn or follow any new direction, stop and listen. What more can I say?"

"Right." Raza flicked his tail flukes. "First I head southeast, then due west into the endless sea where my first sounds began. And if nothing happens there, I'll swim northwest, hugging the outermost coastline....Squee, whee...you won't come? They say those rocky cliffs that face the setting sun grow grass and flowers beyond the wildest dreams."

Flora's head drooped and the feathers on the back of her neck shook, as in a storm. "The sound is beautiful, too beautiful. Now go...quickly, quickly and don't look back until you are far out at sea. Farewell...farewell."

For an instant Raza floated motionless on the surface, then dove straight down. Not a bubble or ripple was left. Jesse and Merle climbed to the highest point of the headland, but they couldn't see him. Merle spun around, waving her arms. From the channel came an answering spout—one, two, three times.

"Jesse, Merle..." It was Norm hurrying down the trail, crunching through the salal.

Jesse covered his face with both hands. If he could only run away or turn into a stone on the trail.

Merle tried to pull his hands away. "Uh, uh, Jesse. Pul-eese."

"So there you are," Norm called out. "I got worried when I didn't find you in the cabin, Jesse. I've been looking everywhere. I spotted the whale and the goose swimming out here and I took the hint from them. How's your head?"

Jesse took a deep breath. "Okay."

Norm sat down beside them. "The whale's gone, has he? Well, I suppose it's for the best. The cove was too small."

Jesse nodded, still trying to hold his breath. It finally burst out. "I'm sorry, Dad...about the boat and everything."

"The boat? Never mind, Jesse. It was getting old and some of the rivets were popping. We need a bigger boat and engine now that we'll be doing more travelling."

"What do you mean, Dad?"

"Remember my promise about taking you out fishing and going up one of the big mainland inlets? And it won't be long before you're taking the boat out by yourself. I guess you got enough experience yesterday for a lifetime, didn't you Jesse?"

Jesse lowered his eyes and nodded.

"I talked to Mr. George this morning and he says the

water taxi can take you both to school. What do you think of that, Merle?'' Norm patted her head.

"Thanks a lot, Dad,'' Jesse replied.

Norm stood up. I'm heading back to the cabin to warm some soup for lunch. And it won't be clam chowder. See you in a while.''

"While...while.'' Merle waved.

Jesse shaded his eyes from the sun's reflection off the water and Merle squeezed her eyes half shut like a sleeping bird. Although they could no longer see or hear Raza they knew that surely, surely, he was swimming...over the waves and faraway.